All the Right Notes

a novel

Elliott Andrews

xoxo, Elliott

AMARILLO, TX

Caprock Publishing Group
Amarillo, TX

Copyright © 2021 Elliott Andrews

First Paperback Edition July 2021

For information about bulk, educational and other special discounts, please contact Caprock Publishing Group.

Caprock Publishing Group can bring Elliott Andrews to your live event. For more information or to book an event, contact Caprock Publishing Group

www.caprockpublishing.com

Cover Design: Brand T Designs
Interior Design: Caprock Concepts
Editing: Brandon Biggers

ISBN: 9781737348719

EARLY PRAISE FOR *ALL THE RIGHT NOTES*

All the

the

Right

a novel

Notes

To Jennifer and Ellie, the greatest loves of my life.

CHAPTER ONE

Rett

The guitars, tuned down a half-step to accommodate my gravelly baritone voice, crunch into a riff that fills the concert venue while a swell of cheers from the crowd rises to meet it. Lights on the stage flash behind the drum kit as the band rips into the first song of our set. I take the stage, guitar slung low across my chest. The Fender Telecaster, once painted a butterscotch blonde but now nearly stripped down to the wood in places, rings out in the mix as I join the song. I take my place in front of the microphone and shout out a welcome.

"How ya doin', Nashville?" I call out.

The response from the crowd is deafening. They're doing alright.

Of course they are.

This is the first concert we've been able to hold in over

a year. An entire album cycle was put on hold due to a global pandemic that shuttered all the bars, all the concert venues.

Nashville went from a happening party town to a ghost town, seemingly overnight.

But now? We're back. The bars have reopened. The mask mandates have been lifted, and we can finally do this again.

I've missed this.

I strum a few chords and begin singing the opening lines of the song. It's the first single from our debut album, and the crowd goes wild with acknowledgement. They are singing along with every word. An anonymous woman's panties fly onto the stage and nearly land on the headstock of my instrument. A wide grin flashes across my face and I turn to Clay, who's holding down the bottom-end of the groove on bass. He shakes his head and mouths a *son of a bitch.*

That's right, Clay.

We're finally back.

* * *

The show went off without a hitch. Nearly two hours later, and after not just one but two curtain calls—hearing a crowd chanting your name, demanding *One more song! One more song!* never gets old—the guys and I are tucked in the dressing room backstage. It's not much bigger than a storage shed, but it's a nice place to cool down and drink a beer or two before we call it a night. I'm drenched in post-adrenaline sweat. My hair, which I let grow out during the pandemic, now feels like a used mop of wavy brown on top of my head. The Nashville Sounds baseball cap that I normally wear is ringed in sweat too. I take it off, run my fingers through my sopping wet hair and put the cap back on.

The four of us have been playing music since our college days. We all met at the University in Murfreesboro. I'm the only one of us not from Tennessee. I spent my entire life surfing the beaches of South Carolina. I moved here to attend college on a music scholarship. Music has always been an important part of my life and I wanted to be a rockstar.

Our band, Rett Gordon and the Last Train Home, is as close to rock as a country band can get. I didn't listen to much country music growing up. Where the other guys in the band grew up on a steady diet of George Strait and Brooks and Dunn, I grew up with Journey, Grand Funk Railroad and whatever else my dad had in the cassette deck of his Wrangler. He was a rock and roll guy, through and through. When Clay and I started the band, we knew we wanted to meld those influences together to make an energetic sound that would tear the roof off a bar but also still be welcomed in the country venues in downtown Nashville.

Clay and I were roommates in college and he introduced me to our drummer, Chris. They had been best friends growing up, and welcomed me into their two-man wolfpack. We gelled almost instantly. The other guitarist, Dave, rounded out the crew. We started out just playing around Murfreesboro and the university campus before making our way up to Nashville. We've been based out of Music City for the last two years now.

When our first self-financed album got the attention of Giant Records, they immediately pushed us back in the studio to have it mastered professionally. Our music was then pushed heavily to the country radio rotations.

Dave is sitting on the black leather couch in the dressing room. I wouldn't go within ten feet of that couch. Unlike a big arena or concert hall, this place has been dingy and dirty since I can remember. There's no telling how many bodily fluids are dried and caked on its surface. He doesn't seem to mind, as he's got a shaker bottle full of green juice parked between his legs.

"You guys don't know how much I've been needing that," he says as he takes a swig from the shaker bottle. I don't see how he can drink that stuff after a show. I need something colder, more carbonated, and preferably alcoholic.

Whereas I let my hair grow out during quarantine, Dave chopped all his off and now rocks the bald-with-a-beard look that makes him look even more badass than ever before.

I grab a Rolling Rock out of the cooler and crack the metal twist cap, tossing it into the Rubbermaid trash can in the corner of the room. The cap bounces off the rim and clatters to the ground.

"Alright, Michael Jordan," Clay says sarcastically. "Think maybe you should stick to music."

I flip him off while taking a swig from the beer. It's ice cold, which is the only way to drink Rolling Rock. "You and me both," I say, turning my attention to Dave. "I was starting to think we'd never get to have actual concerts again. But this…" I trail off.

"I've missed it so much," Chris says. "You can't get that out of acoustic Zoom concerts."

"When the drums started and the crowd out there began cheering, I could feel it in my bones, man," I say. And I could. The ripples of excitement burrowed through my gooseflesh skin and into my very soul. Live music does that. There's just something special about a group of musicians playing together. It's taking four instruments and making magic. It's alchemy.

Clay picks up my bottle cap from the ground and twirls it in his fingers. "I know what you're saying, man. Just hearing that crowd before we even went on gave me chills, dude. I nearly cried."

Of course he did. Clay may be a big burly guy, with a beard that falls nearly to his chest, but don't let that fool you. He's a softie. Like a giant Teddy Ruxpin who happens to play bass.

"Don't say nearly. I saw you. You were straight up bawling, you big baby," says Chris. He's got a metal chair leaned back against the wall and a bourbon and coke in his lap.

Clay chucks the metal bottle cap at him and Chris effortlessly swats at it with his free hand, like a boozy Mr. Miyagi swatting at an incoming punch to the face. The thing ricochets against the exposed brick of the building's back wall and bounces into the trash can. We all look at each other, our jaws wide open.

"That just happened!" Chris jumps up from his chair and lets out a whoop of excitement.

Dave is the least excitable of the four of us. Usually quiet and reserved, but even he nods in appreciation of the bottle cap's aerial gymnastics.

"Toss me a beer," Chris says.

I reach my hand into the cooler and toss him one of the green bottles. He cracks it open and holds it high in the air.

"To us," he announces.

The rest of us join him in the middle of the dressing room, our drinks held high.

"May we do this every night until the last train home," I say.

"Amen," Clay says.

We all drink to that toast.

Damn, it feels good to be back.

CHAPTER TWO

Rett

I wake up the next morning, the sun filtering through the drawn curtains in my apartment. I can hear the hustle of a Sunday morning outside and it just feels so damn good.

For too long, this city was quiet. People holed up in their homes, sheltering in place. The bars were all closed. The only live music was over Facebook Live.

Our label did what they could, but overnight, an entire roster of artists was out of work. Album sales and streams only pay so much. We make most of our money on asses through the doors. The label dropped a few acts, but we were the lucky ones, fortunate to be kept on board.

A few #1 singles off a debut album will do that.

Those dark days are over now. Though it was a hard year, we've come through it on the other side. Just like the sun glowing in dusty rays of light, it's a lot brighter now than it was a few months ago.

I let my eyes adjust to the light. It's too damn early to be up now, but my body does that to me sometimes. It's like it still has some gas left in the tank even after giving it my all on stage last night.

One thing I didn't miss was the smells of the bars after a show. I can smell it on my sheets still, stale cigarette smoke lingering. I figure I'll get up, wash off in the shower and walk down to the cafe on the corner.

I'm surprisingly not hungover, which means I'm off to a good start today. Nothing pisses me off more than waking up with a pounding headache, which happens more and more the older I get. When we were in college, the guys and I could party all night and wake up as fresh as babies the next morning. Now, a hangover is a two-day affair of greasy Mexican food, Tylenol, and sunglasses.

Despite the warmth and comfort of my bed, I get up, letting out a big yawn and stretch. I forgot how a show like that is almost like an athletic event. My muscles ache. My apartment has an amazing view of the Nashville skyline and I open the curtains all the way to let the morning in, seeing people down on the streets below, the buildings glowing in the sunrise. It's an inspiring thing to wake up to every morning.

After a few minutes, I'm in the shower. I can smell the cigarettes, sweat and booze washing off and draining beneath my feet, swirling down the pipes.

After my shower, I throw on a pair of jeans, my boots

and a white t-shirt. As I walk out the door, I grab the black softcover notebook on the kitchen counter. It's got all the song ideas I've ever written, its tattered cover holding within years of work and love. This is the perfect morning to sit outside under the shade of a tree and work on some songs. I'm feeling especially inspired. It's amazing what getting back into your element can do for us creative types.

I've always been this way, too. Writing songs and playing in bands since I was fourteen years old. Now, close to thirty, I still get romantic about my work, my art. Country music was definitely a shift for me, but I found my groove with the guys in the band. We all had the same vision that we still wanted to rock out, even if our brand of rock has a little Nashville twang to it.

The audiences love it, and that's all that really matters to me.

With my notebook in my hand, I take in the morning. It's cool, but not cold. There's a little humidity in the air, which makes it feel like the aftermath of a good thunderstorm. The sun is shining in the blue sky above and it's all making the cogs of my songwriter brain turn.

Perhaps it's finally being able to play live shows again, but I'm feeling pumped. I'm ready to get something caffeinated and spend the morning with my notebook and inspiration. I need to get down everything that's already churning in my head.

A voice behind me pulls me out of my thoughts and I turn to hear someone calling my name.

"OMG, it is!" the young woman says. "It's him! It's Rett Gordon!"

If I had to throw a dart, I'd say she's about twenty-one years old. She's got long dark hair that falls in ringlets around her shoulders. She's in a pair of tight leggings and a Vanderbilt hoodie that's been cut into a sort of crop top. She's accompanied by another girl, this one with long blonde locks. Same age. Same uniform.

"Hi," the brunette says. "Oh my god, I can't believe," she trails off, huffing and trying to catch her breath.

"We're big fans," the blonde girl says.

"Well, thank you very much." I smile and feel like they might both pass out right here on the sidewalk.

"Do you think we could get a selfie with you?" the brunette asks.

I agree and they each perch themselves on either side of me. Brunette takes out her iPhone and gives the camera duck lips while the blonde smiles wide.

Then the brunette turns and plants her lips on my cheek as she snaps another picture. This won't do anything positive for my image, but I chalk it up to free advertising.

"Thank you so much," the brunette says. "We're huge fans."

"Did you come out to the show last night?" I ask.

"Of course!" both girls say in unison.

"It was awesome," the blonde says. "And, oh my god, when you played 'The Sound of Your Heart' at the end, I literally died."

I stop myself from making a joke. The improper use of "literally" really bugs me, but I let it slide.

"I've been waiting for that show for, like, ages," Brunette says. She's no longer looking at me, though. She's got her head craned down to the screen in her hands as she furiously types away at hashtags. I'm sure I'll be tagged in the picture on Instagram. The guys are going to give me shit, I already know.

"Alright, ladies, thank you so much," I say, as I begin to back away.

"No, thank you!" Blondie calls out.

I turn and continue walking to the cafe on the corner of 8th and Broadway. It's busy this morning, especially for a Sunday, but given the nice weather, it's to be expected. After the pandemic, I think a lot of people no longer take for granted the ability to get out and enjoy the city around them. It's easy to get complacent, but if the pandemic has taught us anything, it's that our entire world can be turned around in a single day.

The cafe is hustling and bustling with life. I love it. I notice a few eyes look my way and I give a courteous nod to a pair of women sitting at a corner table.

Waiting in line, I eventually walk up to the front counter and order my usual—a London Fog with extra vanilla. The barista, a young woman with a pixie haircut and a ring through her nose, smiles as she hands me the drink. I feel anonymous, which I enjoy, even for just a few moments. As The Last Train Home has received more and more media attention, I've found fewer places I can just hang out. Even now, this one is going to the wayside of my newfound celebrity status.

After I grab my drink from the bar, I take the paper cup outside. The tea radiates heat into my hand, a comfortable warmth. There are a few tables beneath the awning out here. There's a guy in a suit staring at a laptop. He's got a vein about to pop out of his forehead. A woman with heavy bangs and glasses is sipping on an iced coffee and reading a book. I take a chair at a vacant metal table in the shade of the awning, deposit my belongings and sit down.

With my notebook open, I put the pen to the page and…

Nothing.

Just like the last few months.

The words just aren't coming. I was hoping that our performance last night would reawaken this part of me, but nope. I was wrong. The blank page stares back at me. I flip through, reading some of my earlier writings. Some of it is okay, but honestly? It feels stale. I don't like it. It's the same small-town country lyrics that I've always written.

I turn back to the blank page and lay the pen down. The blue ink seeps into the paper, creating a perfectly round blot. That's the most action it's seen in while.

This sucks.

A blank mind is a blank page. I hear a voice, and it's not mine.

"Hi, um," a woman says.

I look up and see a head of light blonde hair and soft facial features to match. She's tall and gorgeous, with round cheeks and a dazzling smile.

"I'm so sorry to bother you," she says, "and I feel really dumb for asking. But are you Rett Gordon?"

I've never been more happy to be interrupted. I wasn't writing much as it was. "That's me," I say.

"Okay good. I saw you over here and I hesitated because I didn't want to make it weird." Her voice is quick, but it's apparent she's trying not to freak out on me. "I just wanted to tell you that I'm a huge fan. I have your first record, the indie one before you guys got signed. I listened to it during all of my undergrad."

"Well, thank you so much." I'm flattered. "Did you go to Middle Tennessee as well?"

"I did," she said. "But I finished my Bachelor's the year you guys put out that record. I moved here to finish my Master's at Vanderbilt."

As she talks, I can't help but stare. She is stunning. And, it sounds like she's also really intelligent. A tall blonde with an education? Sign me up.

I hold out my hand. "I'm Rett."

She sort of shakes her head and grabs my hand in hers. "I know." She smiles wider. "I should have introduced myself, I'm so sorry," she says. "I'm Stacy."

"Hi, Stacy." I can't help but hold her gaze, her caramel eyes are flaked with specks of green and gold. I could stare into them all day.

A shuffling of chair legs on concrete behind me rips

my attention away from Stacy. I turn to see the woman who was sitting at the table behind mine haughtily grab her belongings and storm off. As she passes by, I hear her mumble something about "fan girls."

I shake it off, and return back to Stacy. "Would you like to join me?" I ask.

"Oh, no," she says, stepping back. Her cheeks have turned a bright red and she averts her eyes. "I have to head back to help my roommate with something. Anyway, it was nice to meet you, Rett."

"You, too Stacy." I watch as she walks away, dumbfounded.

I'm back alone with my notebook, looking down at the blank pages, letting out a sigh.

If there was any chance I'd get some lyrics to come out today, it was totally shot down now.

CHAPTER THREE

Rett

The next morning, I get up early for a meeting downtown at the label. Clay is supposed to meet me here at my apartment. I have enough time to fit in a shower and a shave. Polishing myself up for management. The sounds of The Olympians spill out of my Sonos speakers in my bedroom, filling the space with groovy R&B. Though we write and play country, I still listen to an eclectic range of music, and I've found myself exploring different genres over the last year.

The fog in the bathroom mirror slowly recedes as I finish shaving my neck, but I leave the stubble on my face. If I go completely clean-shaven, I look like I'm thirteen years old.

I walk out of the bathroom, drop the towel to put on my jeans, and hear a yelp.

"No!" Clay shouts as he covers his eyes. "I did not want to see dong first thing this morning!"

I shriek as I gather the towel and wrap it back around my waist. "What the hell! Why didn't you tell me you were already here? I know you can knock!"

"I didn't know you were butt-ass naked!" Clay says, his hands still over his eyes. "Oh man, I'll never unsee that."

"Well next time, make some noise or something. Damn."

With Clay's back turned, I quickly exchange the towel for my jeans and I throw on a white t-shirt.

"Okay, I'm good."

He faces me and lets out an exaggerated sigh. "I yelled for you when I came in through the front door. I didn't realize you didn't hear me." He stops and listens to the music coming from the speakers. "This is funky. What is it?"

"The Olympians," I say. "Just something I found on the internet. Looking for new sounds, new inspiration."

"Nice." He hands me a Starbucks coffee cup. "Grabbed these on the way over."

I take a sip. Hot caramel macchiato, the bitterness of the coffee working against the sweetness of the caramel. It's perfect.

He takes a seat in the leather chair by the window. "So what's this meeting about?"

I head back into the bathroom to fix my unruly hair. I throw some leave-in conditioner and run my fingers through it. These humid Nashville spring days can warm up quickly and it makes my hair a mess. I am halfway inclined to chop it all off one day, but I admittedly like how long I've let it get over the last year. I didn't cut it during the pandemic, and now it falls in wavy sheets to my chin.

"The label wants to talk about our next record," I say. "They want to run some ideas by us, as songwriters."

"We haven't even gotten a chance to properly tour the last record," he whines. "Even now, they're keeping us on the local circuit. For what?"

I emerge from the bathroom and put on a white button-up from the hanger on the doorknob of the closet. I roll the sleeves up past my forearms, letting the Pleiades tattoo on my left arm peek through. I got it when we were still in college, the stars in various hues of red and blue striking across the inside of my forearm toward my bicep.

"I know, but they want to make a big splash now that people are finally able to get out again. We'll get a chance to make a new record and tour new music at the same time," I say. "We're lucky to still have a contract."

"Yeah," Clay concedes.

We leave my apartment. His Tacoma is parked on the curb and I hop in the passenger seat. It's typically a quick drive into the business district, less than three miles south of where I live, but traffic is awful this morning. We should've probably walked, but with as humid as it's been this spring, we'd both be drenched in sweat by the time we reached Giant Records.

As Clay drives, we listen to some of the demos that we've recorded over the last few months. The melodies are great, but I still haven't been able to write lyrics for any of it. In a way, I feel like I'm letting the band down. I'm supposed to be the lyricist for this group, but I haven't written anything new since last winter.

Clay parks in the garage across the street from the building. Giant Records is in one of the skyscrapers in downtown Nashville, a monolith of glass and steel right on the Cumberland River. There are boats out on the water, barges and transports. We cross the busy intersection at Broadway and make our way into the building. The elevator takes us up to the twenty-fifth floor, where we are greeted by the Giant Records logo etched in steel behind the receptionist's desk.

The record label is owned by one of Nashville's most prominent and wealthy families. The Van Hope Group owns not only the record label, but also a television station, and a promotional company. Everything they do is over the top and exquisite, which is reflected in the office. The entire place is pristine and modern, with glass and chrome accents everywhere. The floor is stained concrete and it reflects the lights from the fixtures above. I've seen several of our contemporaries come in and out of those doors. One of country's hottest singers, MacKenzie Taylor, has been Giant Record's lightning star, the darling of the music scene, which I'm hoping is the trajectory for us as well. We're still in smaller concert halls. MacKenzie is playing arenas now. Our largest show had five thousand people. MacKenzie's had over thirty thousand, and she was the headliner.

"Mr. Gordon!" the receptionist says cheerfully. She's got long red hair, and a smile that stretches from dimple to dimple. "They're waiting for you in the conference room now. May I get you something to drink?"

"Hi, Calysta. I'm good for now, thank you."

She turns to Clay and he shakes his head without a word. His face is bright red. I begin walking to the conference room directly ahead of us.

After we're out of earshot of Calysta's desk, and her attention is elsewhere, I slow down and nudge him. "When are you going to grow some balls and ask her out?"

"What are you talking about?" I appreciate his attempts at pretending that I don't see how he gets every time he's around her. In fact, I'm pretty sure the only reason he's tagged along with me is to steal an opportunity to look at Calysta Stephenson.

"You know what I'm talking about. Every time you look at her, you go deer in the headlights. Just ask her out already."

"No way, man. Look at me." He gestures with his hand. "I look like this. And she looks like...that."

"The worst she could say is no," I point out.

"No, the worst she could do is laugh in my face."

I huff as I open the substantial frosted glass door to the conference room. We walk in, and a group of executives are already in there, sitting around a rectangular mahogany table. Their suits are making me feel decidedly underdressed. I should have at least put a jacket on.

Nonetheless, we are greeted with smiles and handshakes. Our A&R representative, David, motions for us at the end of the table. He's young, barely out of university himself, but he's already signed several artists who have been able to catapult from Giant Records onto larger contracts. I wouldn't be surprised if he gets sniped by Universal Music Group or Sony in the near future.

"Good morning, guys," he says. He looks like an intern compared to the rest of the people in the room, but I know he commands their respect as he's been a goldmine of talent scouting. "I have been hearing great things about the show at The Blue Room."

"It was a fantastic show," I say.

"You guys sold it out, again." He smiles.

"Well, I think part of that is the ability to finally play shows again," I say.

"Well," he leans in close, lowering his voice, "I also hear that some guys from Republic were there. And they liked what they saw."

My eyes go wide. If we got signed to a big label like Republic, our entire world would open up. Instead of Broadway concert venues, we'd be in arenas and auditoriums all over the country.

"That's," I start, "that's good. Right?"

"Yeah it is. But we've got to get this next record ready before anything like that can happen."

I nod in agreement, understanding his meaning. Unless another record label is willing to buy out our Giant Records contract, we're obligated to give them at least one more album.

Our manager, James, struts over and joins in the conversation. His suit is tailored, but his hair, slicked back, and shining under the overhead LEDs in the drop ceiling, makes him look like a used car salesman. "You guys talking about the Blue Room show?"

"We sure were," David says.

"Great show," James says. "Great show. It's all anyone can talk about this weekend. Saw a damn good writeup in the *Gazette* Sunday morning too."

I look at Clay. He shrugs in return. "First I've heard of it," I say.

"Well," David says, pulling out a chair at the table. "Have a seat. We'll get started."

I thank him and sit down, with Clay to my right. Everyone else in the room, some of the record execs that I've met a handful of times, all begin to take their seats as well.

At the head of the table, Laura Van Hope pulls her chair up and fidgets with the glasses on her face. She's the president of Giant Records. I've met her exactly once. The fact that she's here means we're either in trouble or there's good news coming our way.

I've often heard from David, that if she's in the room, it means someone's getting canned. I gulp.

"Good morning everyone," she says, and everyone

settles into place. "We have some things to go over budget-wise for Q3 and Q4, but let's get down to business with the first item on the agenda." As she talks, she flips through a stapled stack of papers in front of her. She looks up at me.

"Mr. Gordon, it's very nice to see you again." Her smile is tight-lipped.

I nod. "Thank you, you as well."

"As you know, we're preparing the next cycle for your group, with a new album projected by the holidays of this year."

I gulp. That would be a quick turnaround, even in a perfect world. Nine months to record and prepare an entire record, and even though we've got several songs ready to go, I don't have lyrics for any of them. "That's an ambitious timeline," I say.

"We think you have the fanbase and the *it factor* to become one of our best-selling acts. The first album was a good introduction, but we think, with some fine-tuning, we can turn you and your band into household names."

I turn to David and then to James. Household names? What does she expect? For us to be the next MacKenzie Taylor or something?

It sounds really enticing, but I haven't told anyone — not even Clay, who is sitting right next to me, silent — about my writer's block.

David speaks up, "When I first saw you guys playing at the Iron Pig, I knew you had that special image and unique sound that would make you staples in country ra- dio. Even though *Under the Deep Sky* was a nominal hit, we—Giant Records—believe that we can turn that up a notch. Take what worked on the first record and tweak it until we have a full album of hits."

"Yeah, but it took me damn near ten years to write those songs on that album. You're asking me to do that again, but in six months," I say.

"We've been working on a handful of songs for the next record," Clay adds. I turn to him, and I'm sure my expression of horror gives away the inner panic I'm feel- ing.

"But none of them are close to being complete," I in- terject.

"That's okay," Ms. Van Hope says. "That's actually why we've brought you here this morning. We want you to work with someone outside of the band to write the new record."

As I try to process what she's saying, the conference room door opens and Calysta pokes her head through. "Ms. Van Hope," she says, "Miss St. John is here."

The record exec's eyes go wide with joy. "What im- peccable timing," she exclaims with more exuberance than I'm comfortable with. Ms. Van Hope waves her hand, beckoning the newcomer. "Have her come in. We were just getting to the details."

Calysta nods and holds the door open as another woman walks in.

Petite with long mahogany hair and bangs that fall

down to her eyebrows. A hint of a tattoo showing on her wrist. A pair of black-rimmed glasses above her high cheekbones frame bright amber eyes. I actually have to avert my eyes because I find myself almost gawking.

She looks oddly familiar too, but I can't quite place where I've seen her before.

Then it hits me. And I groan.

CHAPTER FOUR

Nico

"I'm so sorry that you had to start without me," I say, as the receptionist holds the door open for me. "My Uber driver took a wrong turn." I walk in and look for an empty seat at the conference table. I catch him, the singer, staring at me at first and then looking away. I probably shouldn't have stormed off from the coffee shop yesterday morning, but the entire scene was just sickening. I couldn't sit there with a straight face while grown women fawned over this guy just because he can play a guitar.

I politely nod at him as one of the record company's employees pulls a chair out for me. I sit across from Rett Gordon, the front man for his eponymous band, Rett Gordon and The Last Train Home.

I've had his music on my Spotify list for the last few weeks as part of my research. It's the kind of music that attracts the lowest common denominator. It's pickup trucks and hometown heroes and girls and beer. The band had a concert at one of the more prestigious venues on Broadway, and I showed up for just a few minutes of it, standing in the back of the hall.

I catch him staring at me again, and I can tell that he recognizes me from yesterday from his furrowed brow. Granted, I was not very inconspicuous at the coffee shop. Before I committed to this project, I wanted to see him away from a stage, away from the flashing lights and the women screaming his name.

It wasn't much different.

The problem is, he's very attractive. And I'm sure he knows it. His brown hair falls in wavy sheets tucked behind his ears. He's naturally tanned, the kind of warm skin you only get from working under the sun. There's a collection of tattooed stars racing up the inner part of his left forearm. I catch myself counting them.

I don't know if I can do it. This is not where I saw my career going.

Laura Van Hope pulls me out of my staring contest with the singer.

"As I was saying," she says, "We have a lot of faith in the future of you, Mr. Gordon, and we believe that with a little coaxing and with some help on the songwriting front, we have an opportunity to make your next record a smash hit."

The man next to me, just another middle-aged suit-wearer, clears his throat. "Looking at the streaming and download numbers from the first album, it's clear that, despite the songs released as singles, the biggest draws were the non-single cuts. Specifically, the ballads."

The singer huffs. "Well, yeah the ballads were streamed more. They're ballads. But we're not just about that. We want to write songs that people can groove to."

James continues, ignoring the singer's statement. "We want more of that on this new record. We want an album full of singles, and that's where Nico St. John comes in." He turns to me.

Ms. Van Hope nods. "Miss St. John was most recently a writer-in-residence at Southern Methodist University in Texas. She is a candidate for poet laureate. Her poetry has won accolades and awards all over the world. With her help, we'd like for the Last Train Home to write your next record, together."

"I write all my own songs," the singer says through his teeth.

"Really?" Ms. Van Hope's tone is curt. "I think you write what we, the people who sign your paycheck, tell you to write."

He shifts uncomfortably in his seat. I know that look on his face. As sure of himself as he is, as much attention that he receives, there's no hiding the fact that he's battling writer's block. The way he let anything and anyone take his attention yesterday. The way he let the pen rest on the page, unmoving.

"Consider this a sort of science experiment. Your job is to write songs that sell. Our job is to sell your record, and frankly, make a return on our investment in you," Ms. Van Hope continues. "Now, I understand you have music written. We want demos of the potential songs within three months."

"Three months?" Gordon says incredulously. "You can't be serious."

"Very serious, Mr. Gordon. The music industry is an industry. Those who can't keep up get left behind. We certainly don't want that for you. We believe in you, but we know that this partnership will put you on the next level. We need Rett Gordon and The Last Train Home to catapult to the top of the charts and to be a household name."

Gordon looks at me and purses his lips. "I write my own damn songs," he says again.

It's a long and quiet ride down from the twenty-fifth floor. Gordon and the bassist don't say a single word to me. I get it, that was tough news to take, but I don't see why I'm getting the cold shoulder? I'm trying to not take it personally, and also, I don't have time to deal with a grown man licking his wounds.

"Look," I say, breaking the silence. "This is a job for me, not a passion project. I was hired by Giant Records to help you write a record, so don't take it out on me if you feel slighted by them."

"Like I said before, I do this myself," he says, looking forward. "I always have, always will. I don't need you or anyone else."

"Oh yeah?" I interject. "I saw your notebook. It's just *filled* to the brim with ideas. I could barely make out any of the words in there."

He gives me a death stare. At least he's acknowledging my existence now.

"What is she talking about, Rett?" the burly bassist asks. He stands leaning against the back wall of the elevator.

"Yesterday morning, I was at Palace Coffee on Sixteenth. This," he looks at me, "contractor, gun-for-hire, whatever, was...what were you doing? Spying on me?"

"Not spying. Just getting a feel for who I'm going to be working with for the next six months," I say. "I was not impressed."

"Impressed?" he huffs. "Sorry I don't adequately meet your expectations."

"I do expect you to have something written," I retort.

The elevator dings and the doors slide open. A group of suits wait for us to depart so they can go about their day. Rett steps out first and shoulders through the people trying to get on the elevator.

"Excuse us," I say politely as I follow Rett through the lobby of the building and out into the morning sun. It's warm already, with a few puffy clouds mixing with the blue of the sky. It's one of those mornings that feels like thunderstorms are imminent for that evening. I like the way it reminds me of thunderstorm mornings back in Texas.

Even the burly guy is having a hard time keeping up

with Mr. Fit-Throwing. I'm immediately regretting the decision to be part of this country music science experiment.

We haphazardly cross Broadway when Rett finally stops near a bench on the sidewalk.

"Look," he says, whirling around to face me. "I know you're just doing your job, but I just got ambushed in there."

"Good," I say. "Take that emotion and write something down with it. Or, keep ignoring the fact that you're in a rut. Whichever way makes you feel better."

He huffs and spins again, leaving both me and his companion on the sidewalk.

"I'm sorry about him," the burly guy says as he sidles up next to me. "I'm Clay, by the way."

"Nico."

"Cool name."

"Thanks."

"I'll talk to him," he says. "He takes a lot of pride in our music, as I'm sure you can probably understand. That first record took a lot of work. Blood, sweat, tears. You know, the whole shebang. Anyway, I'll get a couple of beers in him, loosen him up. Let me get your number and we can meet up later or something. Maybe things'll be different if we're not in some stuffy board room."

"Yeah, maybe," I say. I give him my number and he punches it into his cellphone. He slips the device back into the front pocket of his jeans.

"Don't take it personally, Nico," he says.

"Oh, I don't," I say.

"Alright, well, I'm gonna chase him down. We'll talk again soon."

He turns and walks off to catch up with Gordon, who is still sulking and huffing down the street. I head the opposite direction. I knew this meeting was going to ruffle some feathers, but I definitely didn't expect this sort of reaction or greeting. If anything, I expected the label and management to be more on my side. They sought me out, after all.

I'll let Clay talk to Rett, but I'm already regretting taking on this project, and we haven't even started yet.

* * *

"Well?" Gabriela asks from the beige couch in the living room. "How did it go?"

"Awful," I say.

Gabriela stands from the couch. She's long-armed and long-legged, with fluid movements that she's developed over the years of modeling. It's not uncommon for me to come home to a living room full of models, all of them head-and-shoulders taller than me. Today, however, Gabriela is alone, apparently watching *The View*, with a plate of avocado toast on the table in front of her.

Alone, that is, except Monster is on the couch with her too. Monster, the tabby cat that we rescued from the alley behind our apartment building. We gave him a bowl of food out on the stairsteps, and he just kept coming back. Like a vampire, once he was invited inside, he took over the place.

He lifts his massive head above the back of the couch – seriously this cat's head is like a Mastiff's – and gives me a disapproving once-over before settling back down onto the cushions, curled in a ball of hate and malcontent.

"What happened?" she asks, leaning against the wall, her arms crossed. She looks very motherly, like she's asking me who hurt me on the playground at recess.

"The Rett Gordon of Rett Gordon and the Last Train Home is an immature man-child, that's what." I set my shoulder bag down in the entryway and remove the coat I'm wearing, hanging it on the hook by the door.

She raises her eyebrows and purses her lips. "That bad, huh?"

"He literally stormed out of the meeting," I sigh a little. "It was the most ridiculous thing I'd ever seen from a grown man. He may as well have thrown himself on the ground and pounded it with his fists like a baby throwing a fit."

"So you're not going to work with them then?"

I know what she's really asking. If I'm going to let this opportunity slip away just because the client is difficult. Not only the opportunity, but the money that comes with it. I've told myself for years that I'm not interested in writing or my art for the money. I would do this for sunshine.

But sunshine doesn't pay the bills.

And I can't afford to let another opportunity slip

away. Literally, I can't afford it. At this rate, if something doesn't go in my favor soon, I'm going to have to find the closest coffee shop that's hiring. One that Rett Gordon doesn't frequent.

Or, I'll have to tuck my tail between my legs and go back to Montana.

Missoula is the last place I want to be.

"It was just a shock, I'm sure. I mean, imagine if it were the other way around. I'd be pretty upset too." I stop myself. I can't believe I'm actually sticking up for him after the way he treated me.

Gabriela, unfortunately, has caught on. A smile creeps across her face. "So is he as cute in person as he is in those music videos?"

"No," I say flatly. *Lying, straight through my clenched teeth.*

The truth is completely different. Because he's very handsome. An ass, and immature, but gorgeously handsome. It's no wonder that Giant Records wants Rett Gordon to be their next big hit, their next household name. That man's face alone would sell a million records.

"Uh huh," she says.

"Why are you still home?" I ask, changing the subject. "I thought you had a photoshoot or something this morning?"

We move out of the entryway and to the kitchen. I take a mug from the cabinet and prepare a K-cup in the coffee maker.

I notice that Gabriela takes a seat at the kitchen bar gingerly.

"Are you okay?" I ask.

"It's this stomach pain again," she says. "I had to re-schedule with Raul for later this week. I just need to rest for a few days."

"You need—"

"I know," she cuts me off. "I need to go see the doctor. But I just haven't had time. I'll go after the show this weekend, I promise."

"You better," I scold, gently. The coffee maker spurts and finishes pouring. I take the steaming mug in my hands.

"What about you?" she asks. "What's on your agenda today?"

"I need to apply for positions at universities. There's a writer-in-residence opening at Tulane."

"You're thinking about leaving Nashville already?"

"I mean, yeah," I say. "The only reason I'm here is because of Giant Records. I don't want to be a song-writer. I want to get back into academia. This is just a layover."

"Yeah, but after Texas…" she trails off and I avert my eyes.

I don't want to think about Texas.

But I also don't want to be here either.

Gabriela is sweet to let me live with her. We grew up together, and though our lives and careers took different paths after college, I'm happy that I ended up back here with her, even if it's just a temporary solution for now. I needed something that resembled solid ground, and I wasn't going back to Missoula, a failure.

It's very strange, though, to be surrounded by Nashville's most beautiful models all the time. All of them, all at least a foot taller than me, have always been super sweet to me. I am sure it's because Gabriela told them about Texas.

"Texas isn't the end of my career," I say.

"I know it's not. I want to see you happy." She smiles and I can see the pain in her eyes as she hides a grimace.

"And I want you healthy," I say.

"After the—"

"After the show, I know. But you better go. Promise me."

"I promise," she says with a nod.

I take my coffee and grab my MacBook and mentally prepare myself for this Tulane application. Taking a few deep breaths, I clear my thoughts and concentrate.

It helps keep my mind off Rett Gordon.

CHAPTER FIVE

Rett

"You're an ass, I hope you know that," Clay says as he takes a swig from his mug. The beer leaves white foam on his mustache and he wipes it away with his forearm.

"Why am I the ass?" I ask.

We're sitting on the patio of M.L. Rose, one of my favorite burger joints downtown. The speakers mounted to the roof out here on the warm patio are pumping the newest MacKenzie Taylor song. It's got a nice groove to it; completely different from her last few country records.

There are a couple of empty mugs in front of us already and Clay is going to town on a basket of cheese fries. The patio is busy for a weekday afternoon. There are a couple of ridesharing scooters leaning on each other outside. I've been antsy for the city to wake back up like this, making music of its own, and it feels so glorious. To be able to just hang out like this, without worrying about masks, social distancing, quarantines, or any of it. Lifting restrictions not only opened up our city, it freed up precious headspace to think again, to create again. It feels like normal life is finally back, after over a year of everything being upended.

We've been here for a couple of hours now, and I'm just starting to relax. The beer helps.

"Because, you threw a goddamn fit back at Giant."

"One, I didn't throw a fit. Two, can you blame me? They want to control the next album. I don't want that. We write our own music. We did it with the first album, and that one was just fine," I argue. I take a bite from my burger and continue my argument between chews.

"You disgust me," Clay says as a glob of habanero sauce plops onto my metal tray.

"And yet, you still love me." I grin wide, knowing that there's bits of burger in my teeth.

"Stop it, good lord." He turns his head while simultaneously handing a napkin in an outstretched hand.

I wipe my mouth and take a gulp from my beer to wash it down. "There," I say. "Happy?"

"Very much so." He takes another sip from his glass. "Look man, I know that we write our own songs and all that. I get it. But at the end of the day, whether we like it or not, the music business is a business. We knew that getting into it. We signed on the dotted line. We're going to have to make some concessions if we want to continue

packing venues like we did last weekend. Streams and radio spins, man. That's what's going to get asses in the
door."

I want to stand my ground, but I know Clay's right.
When we signed that contract with Giant, we signed onto
their vision for our career. Where we want to make music,
they want to make money. Sometimes, those two wants
clash, though. This whole idea of having Nico St. John
write the record with me is one of those clashes, and I
don't think it's one that can be solved by a pep-talk here
at M.L. Rose.

At the same time though…the burgers here are really
good. And the beer is flowing nicely today. And with each
emptied bottle, I find myself more open to Clay's influence.

Our waitress comes back by, dropping off a few more
fresh beers. Clay takes a bottle and pours it into a frosted
mug that accompanies it. He downs his beer and starts
on the fresh one.

"All I'm saying, Everett," he says, using my full first
name. It sounds paternal, like he's a disappointed dad. "Is
that you just give it a shot. Work with Nico, see what
happens. It can't be any worse than what you've got for
the new record so far."

I look away, aware that he knows my problem. I haven't written a new song in nearly fourteen months. In
the beginning, I thought it was just a little hiccup, and I
blamed it on the pandemic and the way our entire world

shut down. I figured I just needed some time to recalibrate and all of my inspiration, my words, would come back.

It hasn't.

"I've been writing music and songs since I first picked up a guitar," I say. "That was fifteen years ago. I've never dealt with this. I've never had writer's block. I don't know what to do about it."

"You accept Nico's help," Clay pushes. "That's how you get through it. That's what's going to help catapult us. I mean, listen to this song that MacKenzie's got." He perks his ear to the speaker above us. "It's a fucking banger. And you know why? Because they had some pros come in and help tweak it. They're not asking you to give up the songwriting aspect. They're just asking that you allow in some help to polish what you're already good at."

I begin to interject, but Clay holds up a hand. "Look man. I love the shit out of you, but you can be so damn stubborn sometimes."

I shrug. I know he's right, but…

"I don't want to be seen as a sellout," I mutter. "Everything we've done, we've done ourselves. We started in a dorm room for Christ's sake."

"We have to evolve, to keep pushing the envelope," Clay says. "Otherwise, we'll become stale. And you know what happens to stale bands?"

"They break up?"

"Worse," he says. "They hold on to what they're comfortable with for so long, all of a sudden they're playing casinos and dive bars fifteen years past their prime. I don't want that."

I sigh because I know he's right. I take another swig of my beer and nod my head. "You're right man. I'm just so scared of the future. I feel like we get one shot at this thing."

"The future can't be any worse than what we just went through. I never thought we'd see the stage lights again. I never thought we'd hear those crowds again. And I don't ever want to lose it again."

"I don't either."

"Good. So it's settled? Besides, if nothing else, she's cute as hell. Just your type. Brunette. Fiery."

I take another gulp from my beer and flip him off. "I'll work with her. Even though I feel like this was forced on me like a pair of handcuffs." As annoyed as I am with the situation, there's no denying that the poet is definitely attractive, with her cute glasses and dark hair. She looks like a brown-eyed Zoe Deschanel.

"Perfect, because she's walking up right now." He grins and pulls his mug up to his face, hiding a mischievous grin.

"Wait, what?" I turn my head and scan the immediate area, looking for Nico. I don't see her.

"I texted her when you went to take a piss," he says.

I scowl. Of course he did.

Then, I spot her. She's crossing 11th at the crosswalk, a messenger bag slung over her shoulder. I watch, trying not to gawk, as she quickly makes her way across the street. Her dark mahogany hair glints in the shining spring sun, and is pulled up in a bun on top of her head.

Clay waves her over. She approaches our table and Clay stands, pulling a chair up for her.

"Thanks for coming," he says.

"You guys have been here for a while," she observes, examining our table of empty bottles tipped upside down in their metal ice buckets

"Sit, sit," Clay insists.

She doesn't take the chair Clay offers, but the one on the edge of the table perpendicular to me. Setting her bag down, she looks at me and smiles. It's not a friendly smile either. It's one of those smug I-told-you-so smiles.

"So," she says, "ready to get to work?"

CHAPTER SIX

Nico

I'm sitting at my desk completing my Tulane writer-in-residence application, when a message sweeps in from the right corner of my iMac. It's Clay, asking me if I'm busy.

He gives me the details, I gather my bag, and throw my hair into a bun. As I start for the entryway of our apartment, phone in hand calling up an Uber, Monster jumps from around the corner and swipes at my legs with his enormous claws.

"Damnit, Monster!" I hate it when he does that. It's like he's always waiting to attack me. "I don't even know why we let you live here."

"Because you love him and feel sorry for him," Gabriela says as she comes out of the bathroom.

"Yeah, well, I wish he felt the same kind of compassion for me," I say.

"Where ya headed?" she asks.

"I'm going to meet these musicians downtown. Something less formal than the boardroom this morning."

Gabriela grins. "Ooh."

"Stop it. It's strictly professional."

"If you say so." That grin stays on her face, insinuating and ridiculous.

"I do say so."

"Well, tonight is the rehearsal for the fashion show this weekend, so I won't be home until late," she says.

"You're going?"

"I have to. I have to power through."

I feel bad for her, but at the same time, I've been pushing for her to make a doctor's appointment. She's the consummate procrastinator though.

Probably sensing the judgment in my eyes – I've never been good at hiding my emotions – she says, "I'll make the appointment before the show this weekend, I promise."

"You better."

"Okay, bye mom," she says, sarcastically.

My phone dings and my Uber pulls up. I jump in the backseat of the Lexus sedan and, after confirming my destination, the driver takes me downtown.

I see the two musicians from where I'm dropped off at the corner across the street from the bar. I wait for the crosswalk signal so I can make my way over.

When I sit down, poor Rett looks like he's seen a ghost. I watch him take long pulls from his beer. One, two, three, four. The waitress asks me for my order, and I decide on a cheeseburger with bacon and a tall Shiner Bock.

Rett raises his eyebrows. "You're a beer girl," he says. "Like me."

I raise my eyebrows in return. "You're a beer girl?"

Clay giggles and it helps me settle in.

"No, I," Rett stammers, and I can't help but laugh as well. "I just haven't met a woman who drinks Shiner."

"I don't regularly like beer, but when I was in Texas for a little bit, I fell in love with it. So, I'll get it at places that have it on tap out here. It's better than the piss water that they try to pass off as beer everywhere else."

"Right?" he says, shifting in his seat and leaning forward now. "I don't know how many more warm silver bullets I can drink backstage. It's awful."

Clay gives him a look and Rett holds his arms out to his sides. "What? You know exactly what I'm talking about!"

I catch Clay's eyes darting between us.

"So, the first order of business is to get to know you as a person before I can get to know you as a songwriter or a lyricist. What makes you tick? What inspires you? Once we know those things, we can start breaking them down and writing some ideas down."

"God, I feel like I'm seeing a therapist," Rett says.

"It's sort of a therapy, yes," I say. "Whether it's poetry or songwriting, what we're doing – what we're attempting to do – is distill all those little thoughts that happen in your brain and turn them into something other people can cling to."

The waitress drops off my beer, liquid dark with a caramel-colored foam on top. I take a sip, letting it linger on my tongue. It tastes so good.

Dabbing my lips with a paper napkin, I continue, "You've got writer's block and we have to figure out why. Then, we can start work on the album."

"We've got a lot of the music written for it," Clay says. "I can get you demo copies of what we've recorded so far. It's not studio-quality of course, but you can at least get a feel for what we're going for sonically."

"Is that how you guys normally do it?" I ask. "You write the music before you write the lyrics?"

"Sometimes," Clay says.

"Sometimes, I'll get a melody in my head and that will help coax the words out. Sometimes, I'll come up with a few lines or a hook, and we write a melody around it. It's pretty convoluted and there's never one set process."

"I see," I sigh. It sounds incredibly chaotic. "Well, you guys are in control of the music and the melodies. It's my job to help you write the lyrics."

Clay nods. Rett just drinks his beer.

"What? Am I mistaken?" I ask, suddenly defensive.

"No, you're right on target," he says. "I'm just concerned that you aren't going to consider the music itself for the lyrics. Poetry is one thing, Miss St. John. But writing songs, writing a record, it's a totally different animal."

"Giant Records wouldn't have brought me in if they

weren't sure that I can help you write a great record," I say. "That's what I'm here to do."

"I think it's just a marketing ploy," he says.

Clay huffs. "Everett," he starts.

"No, it's fine," Rett interjects. "I'm not saying I'm not going to do it. I don't think I have much choice in the matter. But let's be real. Listen to MacKenzie Taylor's new single. That's what Giant wants from us. They want to push us in a new direction, whether we're up for it or not. The entire industry wants to move toward that kind of sound. But we proved with our first record that we can still write rock-styled country and it still sells."

"They're a record company," I say. "They want to make money and they do that by their artists putting out the best record they can. So, you do your job, I'll do my job, they'll do their job, and everyone is happy."

Clay holds out his hands, exasperated. "That's what I told him!"

"Okay, when's your next concert?" I ask, changing the subject. "I want to come see your process, your energy."

"Friday night, at the Yard." Rett says. "But what does a concert have to do with writing the new record?"

"Perhaps the reason that you haven't been able to write anything new lately is because you've been through a traumatic experience and you're still processing it."

Rett looks at Clay and rolls his eyes. "I didn't know the label hired a psychologist as well."

"Don't be an ass," Clay says, and nods at me.

"Believe me or don't, I really don't care," I say. "But

the fact of the matter is, not being able to play shows, to be in your element for over a year, it affected you, whether you accept it or not. So we need to tap back into your pre-pandemic head and see what we can scoop out."

"You sound like you're the expert in traumatic experiences," he says.

I grab my beer and take another gulp, ignoring the statement. "So, Friday night. The Yard. What time do you go on?"

"Curtain call is nine p.m.," Clay answers.

"Perfect. I'll be there."

CHAPTER SEVEN

Rett

The rehearsal space that we've rented is a loft apartment above a women's boutique just south of downtown, close to one of the small universities that pockmarks the city. Chris will tell you that he wanted it because it's centrally-located for all of us. The real reason though is that there's no shortage of college-aged women who frequent the coffee joint in the retail shops down on the ground level of the building. It's amazing how much coffee he drinks.

We've worked for over a year perfecting the space, making it a place to play and prepare for our shows. We plan on recording the next album here too. The open concept living area has been completely overhauled, and where there should be a sitting area, we have our instruments. Noise-dampening panels are tacked to the wall.

The kitchen has been left relatively untouched. All we

use it for is to stock beer in the fridge. There's some Gatorade too, and a bunch of Dave's weird green smoothie shit that looks more like the makings of a salad to me.

Dave emerges from the bathroom just off the living room – the bathroom that will double as a vocal booth when we get ready to record – and pulls his guitar over his shoulder. He toys with the gold knobs on the black Les Paul.

"I was in there taking a piss," he says.

"Thanks for the play-by-play, Dave," Chris says.

Dave flips him off without looking up from the tone knobs on his guitar.

"Anyway, there I was minding my own business with my hands on my massive –"

"No no no," Clay interjects. "I have enough mental images of penises this week."

Both Dave and Chris's heads pop up, looks of confusion and humor etched across their raised eyebrows. They eagerly wait for Clay to elaborate.

"Numbnuts here didn't knock coming over to my apartment Monday morning," I explain. "Got himself a full show."

"You should have taken a picture," Chris says, sitting at the drum set. He's got his hands interlocked behind his head and he's balancing on the little metal stool that he insists we call his *throne*. "We're gonna need something for the album cover."

"We're not putting my," I gesture toward my crotch, "on the record cover." And then I grin. "It won't fit."

"You're right. The vinyl would have to be the size of an M&M," Chris says.

I flip him off as well.

"Anyway," Dave says, his amplifier humming behind him, "before I was so rudely interrupted by your penis jokes, I have this idea for the bridge of 'Home With You' and I want to try it out. Chris, can you count us off into the chorus?"

Chris nods and clacks his drumsticks together with a "1, 2, 3." I put my ear protectors back in just before the first chords. We tear into the chorus of the song, which then transitions into the bridge with a six-count run down the scale.

As I play rhythm, Dave does this really cool blues riff as we transition into the bridge. It adds a lot of flair and really helps build the bridge as a part of the song instead of just a transition. We play through the bridge, into the guitar solo and the final chorus.

After the song, I pull my ear protection out and let the buds hang around my neck. "When did you come up with that?" I ask Dave.

"It's a lick I've had in my back pocket, and I've had it stuck in my head for the last few days for some reason. When I was taking a piss, I heard 'Home With You' in my head and for some reason, it just fit."

"It's perfect," I say. "Let's run through it again."

'Home With You' was arguably our biggest hit off the last record, and it played on country radio constantly. It's one of the ballads that Ms. Van Hope at Giant Records referred to when she said she wants us to write songs that will get more radio attention. And more radio spins means more downloads, streams, and sales.

Which, I hope, also means packed shows, so they can hear our other songs, not just the radio hits and ballads.

We run through the song again, making sure we're on cue and hit the transitions on beat. The blues riff, with some cool bends to the notes, adds weight to the bridge, which I think it was missing in the studio recording.

"Can we take a break? I need to stretch," Chris says, as he stands from behind his drumkit.

"Sounds good to me," Clay replies.

We've gone through the setlist once already, plus the changes to 'Home,' and I could take a breather as well. I set my Telecaster in its cradle next to my Vox amplifier.

My Nashville Sounds cap is sweat-soaked and I take it off to let my hair fall and dry out. Whenever we take a break, we almost always find ourselves out on the patio that looks down onto the street, bustling with foot traffic. I often wonder if they can hear us, even with the work we've done to the apartment to soundproof and dampen it.

Somedays, I wish the tiny balcony was large enough to play on, to give an impromptu concert to the neighborhood, like The Beatles or U2 did.

Of course, we're not The Beatles or U2, and we'd probably just get the cops called on us.

I sit in one of the rickety metal lawn chairs on the patio, and lean back on its legs. The days are getting warmer.

It rarely gets downright cold here in Nashville – we'll get some snow every now and then – but the warmer weather means spring is nearly in full swing. Every passing day means one less day to get this new record ready to record, and I still don't have any damn lyrics.

Clay slides open the patio door and hands me a beer.

"I hope you're being artistic out here, just soaking in all the inspiration around you," he says. He cracks open a silver bullet of his own.

"I was actually just thinking about it, yeah," I say. "And look, I want to apologize for the way I acted the other day." I look up at him. "I felt blindsided, and I didn't respond with my head."

"Dude, don't sweat it," he says. "You're used to having nearly full autonomy when it comes to your lyrics. We knew going in that Giant – especially with Laura Van Hope running the joint now – would want to have some input into the process."

"I feel like it's more than just having input. I mean, they're trying to steer our sound into something more…" I trail off.

"More radio-friendly?" he says.

"Yeah. Something that sounds like everything else out there."

Dave slides the door open, green smoothie in his hand. "What's up?"

"Talking about the meeting with Giant the other day," I say.

"Oh yeah. Was it as bad as you were thinking?" He

gulps from the shaker bottle. It literally looks like pureed peas.

"Well, we weren't dropped."

"I'd imagine we'd have known that already," Dave says.

Clay takes a big swig from his beer. "The label has hired Nico St. John to assist us with writing the new album," he says.

Dave's eyes go wide. "*The* Nico St. John? As in Poet of the Year Nico St. John?"

"You know her?" I ask. But of course he does. If any of the four of us reads poetry for fun, it's definitely Dave.

"Yeah, dude. I have both of her books. She was a Pulitzer finalist a few years ago." He looks at both of us with disdain, as neither Clay nor I have any clue what he's talking about. "Seriously?" he continues. "You two don't read anything, do you?"

I've personally never heard of her. "I don't read what you read."

"She sounds like a big deal," Clay adds.

I nod. Maybe I should make a stop at Parnassus Books soon and pick up one of her books.

Dave shrugs. "That's cool though. It'll drum up some attention from the media once the press release gets out. So what, is she going to come to rehearsals and stuff? Will she be in the studio with us? When do we get to meet her? Do you think she'll autograph my books?"

All of his questions, as excited as he is, make my head

spin. "I don't really know yet. It's still early in the process." I scratch at the label of my beer, peeling off bits of paint with my fingernail.

"When does the label want the album finished?" Dave asks.

I gulp.

Clay answers. "November."

"You're shitting me!" Dave nearly falls backward. "That's…that's…"

"Nine months, I know," I say. "Six months to write and record, three months of pub and promotion. It's going to be nuts."

Chris slides open the patio door. "What are you bums talking about?"

"The new album," I say.

"Oh, we're just watching Rett sweat over being forced to work with a Pulitzer-nominated poet," Clay says.

"Um, she's got a name. Nico St. John," Dave adds. "And Giant wants the new record ready for a November release."

"One, who the hell is Nico St. John and two – November?! There's no way." Chris's eyes are wide with terror. "We just started writing the music. We have, what? Five, six songs?"

"None of you pay attention to anything around you, do you?" Dave says.

Clay interjects. "It's going to be fine. We'll get the music finished up, Rett and Nico will write the lyrics, and it'll all work out. This time next year, we'll have the biggest record of the year."

"I appreciate your enthusiasm," I say. I wish I shared it.

Chris hands me a brown package. "This was delivered for you," he says.

"Here?" I ask, confused. Why would anyone deliver a package for me here? No one, aside from the band and the management at the label, knows of our rehearsal space. It's our oasis, apart from everywhere else.

I take the package from Chris. The plain brown wrapping is tied with a string, but I can already tell that it's a book.

"Who's it from?" Clay asks.

I shrug. "Who dropped it off?"

"A courier knocked on the door."

There's a folded tag tied to the string. I open it. It reads, *A place to pour your words. Your new album is going to be great.* "It's not signed."

I slip the string out of its knot and tear the brown paper off to reveal a leather-bound notebook. It's got my initials embossed in the bottom right corner of the cover.

"What is that?" Dave asks.

"Looks like a peace offering," Clay says.

Dave looks up at him.

"Him and Nico didn't exactly get off on the right foot," he explains.

Ignoring their back-and-forth gossip about me and Nico, I flip through the empty notebook. The paper feels fine and high-quality. It's not my regular beat-up lyric book, with its frayed faux-leather cover and shitty paper that bleeds with any wet ink.

"What happened?" Dave asks.

"The label kind of ambushed us with her, honestly. But it's not a big deal. They're ready to push for new music and new sales now that the pandemic is over," Clay says. He's always so optimistic, so good at seeing the positive in every situation. It's a trait that I admire and envy.

"We had a misunderstanding," I say, my attention still on the notebook, weighing heavy in my hands. It's a sweet gesture, and I'm sure Nico means well sending it, but it's a bit too much. It's outside of my comfort zone and it immediately sends my anxiety about this album through the roof. I tuck it between my legs on the lawn chair. "But yeah, Nico St. John is going to help write the next album. In the meantime, let's get back to the setlist for tomorrow night."

We go back inside the rehearsal space, the music from our instruments drowning out all of my anxieties.

CHAPTER EIGHT

Nico

"It's fine," Gabriela insists. She's twisting her hair in a heat wand, creating ringlets.

We're in the living room, and there are no less than a dozen six-foot tall supermodels running around the place. The fashion show is tonight, and I'd completely spaced out when I told her that I'd be there. The concert is tonight too. I would much rather be at a swanky fashion show with high-quality hors d'oeuvres than at some country bar full of drunk men and screaming women, but she won't have it.

"You've been to a dozen of these shows now," she continues. "You should know by now they're all the same."

"But they're quieter and not as...drunky."

"Drunky?" She lifts an eyebrow.

"What? Shakespeare made up words all the time, you know."

She smiles as she stuffs her duffle bag with hair accessories. "I didn't really pay much attention to Shakespeare in class."

One of the other girls has her nose nearly pressed to a portable makeup mirror as she applies a wingtip eyeliner.

For the record, I hate wingtip eyeliner.

"We were looking forward to this one. And the tacos afterward," I argue.

Tonight's fashion show is kicking off swimsuit season and hosted by one of downtown Nashville's most upscale boutiques, Dotsy's. There are amazing food trucks that gather in the park just a few blocks from the shopping district. They have some of the best tacos and gyros you can get from a restaurant on wheels. It's half the reason I even go to these shows.

"Just come to the venue after the concert. I'll be ready for late-night snacks after we're done," she says. "I'd much rather swap places with you though."

I laugh. That would be a sight to behold for sure. I've worn heels exactly twice in my life – and a bikini even less. "I think I'm good."

"You'll have to let me know if they play 'Home With You'. I love that song."

"The label wants more songs like it, apparently," I say. "A record of hits."

"That's exciting." She doesn't look up from her bag

as she takes account for her supplies. "You get to be involved with that." She then turns to me with a cat-like grin, eyebrows raised in that fake-flirtatious way. "Maybe you can introduce me to the band."

"A swimsuit model is the last thing they need to distract them right now. But" I pause, "I'm sure it could even be a source of inspiration."

"I swear, if there's a song about bikinis and trucks and beer—"

"It would be just like every other country song on the radio right now?" I cut her off.

That's my biggest complaint about this whole situation. It's not that Rett Gordon isn't a spoiled baby – he is – but that I have somehow found myself as far from academia as you can get. Instead of a writer-in-residence at a prestigious university, or being nominated for poet laureate, I'm here in Music City working with a country music band whose tastes couldn't be further from my own.

It's depressing.

"But that's why they hired you," Gabriela says. "Ever since we were little, you've had a way with words. This is just another rung on the ladder to your dream."

"You're right," I say, feigning my optimism.

"If anything, you get to hang out with a band while recording an album. Do you know how many people would love to be in that position? This could be the start of something even bigger than you imagine for yourself."

Gabriela can always find the positive in any situation. She's the kind of person that looks at the shadows all around and is excited because the sun is shining.

I peek at the time on my phone. "Okay, I've gotta go," I say. "I'll text you. Good luck."

We hug and I leave the bustle of the apartment and step into the cool evening air.

Maybe Gabriela's right. I take a deep breath and commit to enjoying this night.

I mean, despite everything else, I get to go to a concert for free.

* * *

The lights on the stage twist and twirl like a thousand spotlights into the crowd and the bass drum thumps so hard I can feel it in my chest. This is unlike anything I expected a country concert to be. For some reason, it played out in my head as a room full of square dancing and banjos. This is, for all intents and purposes, a rock show. And Rett Gordon is having the time of his life.

I think I might be having a good time myself.

I'm standing backstage, close to the curtains, just off to the side of Clay. Whereas Rett is fully aware of his stage presence, Clay is the stoic foundation of the rhythm section, keeping everything together.

The other two members of the band I only met in passing as they were preparing for the show, but I'm looking forward to working with them too.

I actually can't believe how much I'm looking forward to this project now.

"They put on a hell of a show, huh?" a muffled voice says into my ear.

I jump, startled, but when I turn, I see a friendly face. David, from the label, has sidled up next to me. I've only ever seen him in a suit and tie, but tonight he's in a blue flannel and jeans, with a backwards ballcap. He looks like he belongs in a frat at Vanderbilt, not as one of the most prominent members of Giant Record's executive team. I can see with his sleeves rolled up, his left arm is completely covered in a sleeve tattoo. He's got two beers in his hands and offers me one.

I begin to object, but I see that the can hasn't been opened, so I feel safe. I thank him and crack the tab open. The liquid, not as cold as I'd like it to be, feels good anyway.

"They're really great live," I say.

"When I first saw them, it was at some shitty dive bar in Murfreesboro. Even then, I knew they had it. Know what I mean?" he says.

And I know exactly what he means. I don't know if it's specifically Rett's stage presence or the way these four guys make it sound like there's at least three times that many playing, but they are one of the best bands I've ever heard live.

"How did you get into this?" I ask, having to nearly yell into David's ear.

"I always wanted to play in a band," he explains. "But I can't sing and I've got no rhythm."

I can relate.

"Have you ever heard a song or a band that no one else has really heard yet?" he asks. "And you tell all your friends that they're going to be the next big thing?"

I know what he's talking about. Back in college, Imagine Dragons played at the University of Montana, and Gabriela and I both knew that they would hit it big. That was at least a year before we heard them on the radio.

"That's what I do for a living," he says. "And it's a fucking blast."

I can see what he's talking about. Getting to go to concerts, scouting out potential talent for the label.

"Did you discover MacKenzie Taylor too?" I ask.

"I sure did." He takes another swig of his beer. "Damn, that's been eight, nine years now? She was just a kid at the time, but she's probably the reason I have *carte blanche* with the Van Hopes. I just need these guys here to put out a hit record now."

I don't know if the statement is something he needs personally and professionally or if it's a less than gentle nudge in my direction.

"I feel confident in what we're going to create," I say.

"Good."

From the stage, the band finishes a song, and tells the crowd goodnight. This isn't the end of the show though, because the houselights haven't come on.

The guys come over to this side of the stage. Rett sees me with David. He smiles as he grabs a bottle of water from a cooler on the ground next to the curtains.

"What do you think?" he asks, breathless, like he's ran

a marathon. He's sweaty, his hair glistening in the low lights, and his t-shirt clings to his torso, highlighting his physique. I can see the ripples of toned muscles under the white fabric. He takes a long gulp from the water bottle.

I swallow. "It sounded great," I finally say, unable to stop gawking at his ripped body.

"Another kickass show, Rett," David says. They fist bump, and I can't help but shake my head at the frat boy behavior.

An invasive shiver shoots up my spine and I have to take a moment to collect myself and slow my pulse. I'm not in Texas anymore. *I am safe here.*

"Thanks for coming out tonight," Rett says to me.

I smile, masking the negative thoughts I'm having. I push them back to the hidden compartment in my brain that I keep them in. "Of course," I say. "I need to get a feel for how you guys create, how you make music. You know, to make some progress on the new album."

I have to nearly yell, not because of the music anymore, but because the crowd out in front of the stage are downright screaming for more. Chants of "One more song! One more song!" echo through the entire concert hall.

"You don't have to pretend to always be working," Rett says with a wide grin. "It's okay to just enjoy yourself."

He chucks his now-empty water bottle to the side without even looking and it lands in a Rubbermaid trash can.

"Alright," he turns and says to the band. "Ready to give the people what they want?"

They walk back out onto stage and the roar from the three thousand people in attendance is deafening. The musicians take up their instruments and after a drum count-off from Chris, they play 'Home With You.' I take out my phone and record a twenty-second clip and send it to Gabriela. She responds with three heart emojis.

After the encore, we're all in the venue's dressing room, and the guys are cutting up. I lean against the wall, taking it all in. I remind myself that this is work, that I'm just getting a feel for the band in order to help them write the new record. But honestly? This is so much fun, it doesn't entirely feel like work. No wonder so many boys want to grow up to be rock stars.

"You got plans after this?" Rett asks. I have my nose buried in the screen of my phone. I texted Gabriela to ask when she wanted to hit up the taco truck.

"Oh, I'm just meeting my roommate at Dotsy's."

"Oh that's cool," Rett says. "Does your roommate work for the boutique?"

"No, she's a model," I reply.

The entire room screeches to a halt and all eyes turn to stare at me.

Chris, the drummer, speaks up. "So…" he trails off. "Your roommate is a model who is currently at a bikini fashion show? What the hell are we still doing here?"

My phone dings and it's Gabriela.

Hey girl. This show is running long.
Won't be able to meet up til later.
Hope you're having a good time.

"Well, never mind," I say, as I shut the phone screen off. "The show is running long. So, no hanging out with the models. Hope you'll all survive."

"What about you?" Rett asks.

"What about me?"

"Got plans?"

"Well, I was going to hit up the food trucks on Broadway after this, but now I'll probably just head home."

"No way," Rett says. "That taco truck over there is my favorite. Let's go grab some food, talk about this new record." He flashes that wide grin. I feel like it gets him into a lot of trouble.

It would probably get me into a lot of trouble, if I let it.

I return his smile. "Tacos it is."

CHAPTER NINE

Rett

We're in The Curtain Club's dressing room after the show. As much fun as that first one was, this was somehow even better. I think it's because I know that it wasn't a fluke or a consequence of post-quarantine life, but people are genuinely excited to see us play, to hear our music.

It makes me giddy and nervous. I know they expect a new album this year, and the thought of writing it absolutely terrifies me.

What doesn't terrify me, at least not at the moment, is Nico St. John standing by the door of the dressing room. She and Clay are laughing about something and I can't take my eyes off her. There's no denying that she's adorable, but there's something in the way she smiles, wide and full, it lights up her whole face. And when she laughs, it lights up the entire room.

Clay calls over to me. "Did you notice that?" he asks.

"Notice what?" I'd been so lost in my thoughts that I wasn't paying attention to what they were talking about.

"When Dave nearly fell over his pedal board."

I glance over at Dave, who's on the couch — the dude loves couches — sipping on a smoothie. "No, I didn't. Dave," I call out. "Did you almost eat dirt?"

He looks up from his phone. "Yeah. Went to step on my wah pedal and nearly slipped and fell."

"Maybe you should wear shoes on stage then," I shrug. I'm convinced Dave was born in the wrong era. He would've been right at home in the sixties, with his flared-bottom jeans and running around barefoot, a kale smoothie in his hands.

"No way, my man," he says. "I have my morals."

I laugh and look over at Nico, who's got her phone in her hands, furiously typing out a text message. She doesn't seem to be off in her own world, though. She seems like she's genuinely enjoying herself.

After her revelation of her roommate being a model, and saying she's just going to head home, I suggest going to the food trucks together, and she surprisingly takes me up on the offer.

Now I have to follow through with it, so I thinly veil it as a chance to talk about the new record, but I think anyone and everyone can see right through me. If Nico had any objection though, she didn't show it. In fact, she agreed immediately.

The taco trucks on Broadway are less than two miles

from The Curtain Club, so we decide to walk. Outside, the sidewalks of downtown Nashville are bustling with energy and life. A group of women in a bachelorette party *woo-hoo* as their limousine drives past.

"How's the city treating you?" I ask, as Nico walks in lock-step next to me. We're close, but not too close.

"It's alright, I suppose," she says. "I feel like I'm a long way from home."

"That's sometimes a good thing though, right?"

"Sometimes," she answers. I can tell there's something hidden in the one-word response, something that she's keeping tucked away.

"I'm not from here either," I offer.

"I know. You grew up in a South Carolina coastal town, where you were an award-winning member of your high school choir. You were accepted to Middle Tennessee University upon graduation on a music scholarship."

My eyes go wide. "Okay, stalker."

She laughs. "I'm just doing my job. I have to help you write a record, which means I have to know who you are. And not just the parts that are public record, but who you are when you're alone. What makes that brain of yours tick?"

"I wish I knew," I huff. I haven't felt anything tick in my brain in a long time.

We stop at a crosswalk and wait for the light to turn green to allow us to cross.

"Well, what inspires you?" she asks, as we start to cross the busy intersection.

"Lots of things. The ocean. A field of wheat being cut. The trees of the Cherokee Forest," I say. I used to have no problem writing songs, and not just about boots and trucks and beer. One of the things I love about country music is the ability to tell a story in a song. Whether that story is about a bonfire party or feeling alone in the world, it's still a story, and people find themselves in stories.

We make it to the row of food trucks, and each one has a line a dozen people deep. The taco truck, El Giro, has double, if not triple.

"Might as well get in line," I say with a shrug.

"So what do you think it is that's keeping you from writing?" she asks as we take the caboose of the line.

I chuckle. "If I knew that, perhaps I wouldn't need you." The words come out harsher than I intend, and I see her response to them, inaudible but still struck across her face.

That adorable, pensive face.

"I'm sorry," I backpedal. "I didn't mean for that to come out that way. What I mean is, I still see those things. They still move me. But I don't know. Something just feels…missing."

She looks up at me, her eyes, honey hazel and full of congruency and understanding. She doesn't even have to say anything and I can tell that she understands what I'm talking about.

"Like perhaps the last year took something from you?"

"Exactly," I say.

All in all, I know I'm lucky. I'm alive. The people around me are still here. We didn't lose anyone from the sickness that ravaged the world and shut down everything I'd come to depend on. Somehow it managed to still take something from me. Something intangible and as real to me as my own two hands.

It stole my passion. My ability to see the world, its beauty all around me, and use that to create music. It's a hard thing to admit, that I let it happen or maybe I didn't notice, in the chaos of it all. But it's gone, I've lost it, and I haven't the faintest idea of how to get that part of myself back.

"It's okay to feel that way. And perhaps we can harness that desolate feeling and transform it into something hopeful."

"You're really good with words," I say. "Obviously."

"I've been writing for a long time," she says.

The line moves and we step forward. We're nearly to the front and I can already taste the barbacoa. "El Giro makes the best tacos I've ever had. I swear, I could eat a dozen and still want more."

"It's my favorite too. In fact, for the first week I lived here, it's all I ate. They were parked close to our apartment and I'd walk down for dinner."

"So, what made Giant reach out to you, and what made you want to accept? Songwriting is different from poetry, right?"

"My roommate works for the Van Hopes' modeling agency," Nico says. "She was able to get me in the door.

There was a mutual…need."

There's a hesitation there, something that she's not willing to disclose.

She continues. "But honestly? I didn't want to take you on. In fact, if I'm completely honest, I'm not sure that I'm not in over my head here. It's not just my reputation on the line. It's yours, it's the label's."

"You definitely know how to make a boy feel at ease," I laugh. "Whatever it is or was though, I'm looking forward to writing with you. I think it'll get me out of my comfort zone and back into the right headspace. Oh, that reminds me. Thank you for the new notebook."

She looks up at me again, but this time, there's no trace of silent understanding. Her brow furrows in confusion. "What do you mean?"

"You know," I say. "That new notebook you had delivered to our rehearsal space yesterday. It's really nice. I'm almost too afraid to write in it though. I feel like I'd ruin it."

"I honestly have no clue what you're talking about," she says.

"You left a note with it."

Before I can continue, her phone buzzes and she pulls it out of her pocket. She looks at the screen and her face goes death-white, her entire countenance changing in an instant.

"I have to go."

She immediately spins and starts sprinting back in the direction of the venue.

"Wait!" I call out. "What's going on?" I leave the taco line and rush after her.

"My roommate," she says. She's got her phone to her ear now. "She collapsed at the fashion show. She's being taken to the hospital."

CHAPTER TEN

Nico

My heart is pounding out of my chest. I'm standing in the middle of a downtown sidewalk, but I feel myself pacing back and forth, unable to stay still. The phone is ringing in my ear, and finally there's an answer on the other end.

"Nicole," the voice says. It sounds just as panicked as I am.

"Ingrid, what's going on?" I ask frantically. "Is she okay?"

"I don't know. Gabbi was complaining about not feeling well. She was backstage getting ready for the finale when she collapsed. She passed out. The ambulance is taking her to Metro General."

"Do they know what happened?" I'm on the verge of tears.

Beside me, Rett is on his phone. I'm too preoccupied

and frantic to pay attention to him right now.

"I have no clue, but I'm headed up to the hospital right now. Hopefully we can get more answers. Should I call you when I get there?"

I silently curse. I should've made her go to the doctor weeks ago when she started complaining about her stomach pains, but Gabriela is — and has always been — not only stubborn but the world's biggest procrastinator.

"No, I'm on my way. I'll meet you there."

"Okay. I'm sorry," she says.

I want to admonish her for apologizing, but I just say, "It's okay. I'll see you soon."

I hang up the phone and open Uber. There's a rush right now and the nearest ride is over twenty minutes away. I curse again, this time out loud.

"Fuck, fuck, fuck," I say.

"Hey," Rett says. "What's going on?"

"My roommate. She's being taken to Metro General. She's been complaining for a few weeks now about some stomach pains and now she's collapsed at the fashion show and I'm trying to get an Uber and it's not fucking working." I realize that as I'm talking, this vomit of words and profanity spilling from my lips, Rett is cool and collected.

"I've already called Clay. He's bringing the truck. Four minutes out. We'll take you to Metro General," he says. His face is steely and resolute, the face of a man who sees a problem and is two steps ahead of it, finding a solution as quickly and efficiently as possible.

The way he's controlling this situation, helping me, makes me want to bury my face in his chest. Feel his embrace, feel some sort of comfort, anything that will convince me it's going to be okay. I want to break down and let him hold me up. But I can't do that. Not only would it be a serious overstep in our professional relationship, but I also can't let myself break down, because I need to be strong right now. I need to find out what's going on with Gabriela. There's no time for me to come undone.

"Thank you," the words barely escape my lips. I'm both scared at the moment and thankful that he's here with me.

Those four minutes either go by incredibly fast or Clay drives like a bat out of hell because a black pickup truck pulls up to the curb with a squeal of its brakes before I know it. The windows are rolled down.

"Y'all get in!" Clay calls from the cab.

Rett holds the passenger door open for me and I hop inside. The interior of the Silverado's backseat is cramped and it smells like Copenhagen. The radio is blaring initially but Clay turns the dial to reduce the volume.

"Metro General, right?" he says, though he's already driving in that direction, neither Rett – who has opted for the backseat with me – nor I have even had time to fasten our seatbelts.

I confirm our destination.

"Okay," Clay says, "get your strap on."

I look at Rett quizzically as he's clicking his seatbelt. "It's an inside joke," he says. "With the band. It means, put on your seatbelt."

I just shake my head, in no mood for jokes, and click my seatbelt.

Clay's honking the horn and yelling at pedestrians. "Get out of the way! Move!"

Luckily, once we're off Broadway and out of the music district, there are fewer people mingling in and around the streets, and much less congestion to get through.

I feel my palms saturated with a nervous sweat and I wipe them on my jeans. I feel so guilty. Instead of nagging at her for the last week, I should've taken Gabriela to the doctor myself. I should've not let her be so indecisive or procrastinate with something as serious as her health.

Rett reaches across the seat and puts his hand on mine. My head jerks reflexively toward him as my hand pulls away from his touch.

"Sorry," he says, slowly moving his hand away from mine. "You just look really concerned, and I want you to know that it's going to be okay."

"How do you know it's going to be okay?" I spit out. My tone is more pissy than I intend, and I know it's because as scared as I am right now, I'm also mad at Gabriela for not going to the doctor when I told her to.

I take a deep breath.

"I just want you to know that we're here for you. Clay and me both," he says. He's so calm, and despite my initial reaction to his touch, I want him to reach out again, to take my hand. To reassure me, to tell me again that it's all going to be okay.

Clay nods in the rearview mirror and I catch his eye momentarily before he looks back to the road ahead of him. We're getting close to Metro General. I can see the hospital tower approaching.

"Where is she?" he asks. "Emergency room side?"

"Yeah," I nod.

Clay pulls the truck up to the emergency room entrance, the sliding glass doors wide and open, light from the inside spilling out into the parking lot. I thank him and hop out of the truck. Rett gets out as well.

"What are you doing?" I ask.

"Coming with you," he says.

I don't argue. I turn and head for the front doors, with Rett on my heels.

I see Gabriela's friends, impossible not to notice them, looking out of place in an emergency room's waiting area. There are a few families in chairs, reading magazines, staring at screens in their hands. Normal-looking. These girls, though, they all look like, well, like models. As they see me come in, Ingrid stands and extends her arms to me. She's tall, even for model standards, and my head barely comes to her chest as she takes me in her embrace. Her hair, long and red, falls in my face and it smells like hairspray and dried sweat.

"What's going on?" I ask, my voice quivering.

"I do not know," Ingrid says. Her accent is Germanic and choppy. "Gabriela fainted backstage."

"Her stomach," I say. "She's been complaining about some stomach pains for about a week, and I told her to go see the doctor. She was putting it off until after the show."

"Yeah, she didn't look like herself tonight," one of the other girls, Monique, says. Like Ingrid, she's tall, but with dark mocha skin and the most beautiful afro I've ever seen. "Usually she's so vibrant and full of energy, but tonight..." she trails off, but I know what she means.

Gabriela hasn't been herself in a few weeks. I thought perhaps it was the show coming up, just nerves.

In hindsight, I was wrong.

And I'd give anything to go back in time to make sure she was taking care of herself instead of being so caught up in what I was dealing with.

There are a lot of things I would do differently with the gift of hindsight.

"I know," I say. "She's been off for a while now."

Rett has been standing behind me, silent this entire time, not butting in or making himself known. The women are giving me the eye though. *Introduce him*, they all seem to say, nonverbally.

"Ladies, this," I say, "is Rett Gordon. He made sure I got here quickly."

Rett nods.

"*The Rett Gordon?*" one of the other girls asks. I've never met her before, but I recognize her from some of the promotional shots from Gabriela's Instagram feed.

"The one that caught fire to the rug at St. Thomas Church when he was eight years old?" he asks. "That's me."

The cadre of fashion models all laugh.

"You wrote that one song. 'Home With You' right?" she asks.

Rett, for as charismatic as he is, especially on stage, is modest in his response. "Well, it was a group effort. My band, we write the songs together."

"I love that song," she gushes.

"I didn't know you were seeing anyone," Monique says, giving Rett the once-over.

"I'm not. We're working together," I say, too quickly to sound anything but guilty.

"She's helping us with the new album," Rett adds. "The record label hired Miss St. John to assist with the lyrical content."

"Oooh," Monique says. "That's fun." She lifts one eyebrow. I shake it off.

"How long ago did you guys get here?" I ask – both out of concern and also to get the spotlight off of me and Rett.

"We followed the ambulance," Ingrid says. "They rushed her back. We haven't talked with a doctor yet."

"Well, I guess we'll just wait then," I say. I then turn to Rett. "Thank you for bringing me, but I'm sure this isn't how you wanted to spend your Friday night. You can leave if you want."

"Nico," he says, "I ain't going anywhere."

"That's sweet," I say. "But –"

He cuts me off. "But nothing. I'm here with you, and

I'm going to stay here with you until you get some answers and find out what's going on with your friend. Besides," he nods toward the group of Gabriela's cohorts and flashes that million-dollar country boy smile, "I can't leave you here with all these supermodels by yourself."

"Oh, look at you, Prince Charming," I say with an eye roll. "So valiant and chivalrous, to be so concerned about those around you."

He reaches out and takes my hand. Again. His touch sends electricity through my whole body. It's one of those things that I want to instinctively pull away from, but there's something magnetic about him, about his touch. It feels…safe. I don't know what it is or why, but it's unlike anything I've ever felt before.

He smiles again, this time with less of that country boy charm and with a weight in his eyes that feels adoring. "I'm kidding. I'm not leaving you alone."

"I'm not alone—" I begin to argue, but he cuts me off.

"I'm staying right here."

He squeezes my hand gently and releases it.

Behind me, I hear a young child fiddling with the vending machine and calling for his mom to give him money for candy. Rett nods toward the vending machine. "You still hungry?"

* * *

An hour later, stuffed full of Chili Cheese-flavored Fritos,

Famous Amos cookies and Pepsi, Rett and I are sitting in the grey plastic chairs of the waiting room. I could fall asleep at any minute, and I find myself at moments forgetting even why we're here.

The wide doors that lead to the patient area open and a doctor calls out Gabriela's name. I jolt up out of my seat. "I'm with Gabriela!"

Walking over to the doctor, an older gentleman in green scrubs, he's got a look of concern in his eyes and I can feel my gut sink with horror.

"What's wrong?" I blurt out.

I sense Rett and the girls behind me, all of us nearly surrounding this poor emergency room doctor. He's probably never seen a sight like this, half a dozen fashion models in his ER.

"First and foremost, everything is going to be okay," he says. "She may be sore for a few weeks, but the operation went smoothly."

I sigh with relief. "Why did she collapse? What operation?"

"Preliminary blood test revealed a pregnancy. But when we did a CAT scan, we couldn't find a baby in the uterus."

My mind goes completely blank and I zone out of anything else he says.

Pregnancy?! Gabriela was pregnant?!

The doctor continues speaking and I catch the last bit of what he's saying, "...she's in recovery and we'll keep her monitored for at least twenty-four hours before we release her. You're welcome to see her, but" he looks at the cadre behind me, "we're limited to just two visitors in the room."

I look back at the girls and at Rett. "Who's going with me?"

Ingrid raises her hand sheepishly. "I will go," she says.

Rett gives me another one of those reassuring smiles. He went from such a pain in the ass to so completely comforting.

We leave the rest of the group in the waiting room, and as the doctor leads us down the hall, the word pregnant runs rampant through my mind, wondering how this could've happened.

Of course, I know how it happened, but I just don't know when Gabriela was last with a guy. If she was secretly seeing someone, she's been incredibly surreptitious about it.

We reach a recovery room, and the doctor opens the door. It's dimly lit, a welcome difference from the harsh lighting in the hallway. It takes my eyes a moment to adjust.

Ingrid follows me to the hospital bed where Gabriela is lying. Even in the low light, I can see that she's still in full makeup. She makes post-surgery look posh.

She looks up at me with a weak smile. Her eyes are still glassy from the pain meds. There's an IV drip bag beside the bed and the machine beeps occasionally.

"Hey," she says.

"Hey sweetie," I say. I place my hand on her forehead.

"How are you?"

"You tell me."

"Do you remember fainting?" I ask.

"I remember not feeling well. And a sharp pain in my stomach. And then…"

Ingrid approaches the bedside. "You had us so worried. Why didn't you tell us you were pregnant?"

Gabriela's eyes shoot open, with surprise and horror. "I was what?"

"It's okay," I say calmly. "You had an ectopic pregnancy. It wasn't viable, but it had ruptured your fallopian tube. You were bleeding into your uterus." I was trying to remember everything the doctor said, even when my mind went blank.

"What?" is all she can croak, and her glassy eyes begin to fill with tears.

I hold her hand. "It's okay. You're okay."

"But" she starts, "I haven't been with anyone."

I nod. "It's okay," I repeat. Right now is probably not the best time to dump all this information on her or make her try to remember the last few months. She's still hopped up on pain meds.

I change the subject, "Can I get you anything? Water?"

"I need to feed Monster," she answers.

"I'll make sure Monster is taken care of," I say. I can't wait to get mauled by that giant demon cat when I try to open his can of food. He definitely lives up to his namesake.

"How long will I be here?"

"The doctor said they're going to keep you at least overnight. Probably twenty-four hours. But I'll be here with you as much as I can."

"I will be here as well," Ingrid says.

"Thank you." Gabriela leans back into the pillow behind her head and shuts her eyes.

A nurse walks in, startled to see us in here with Gabriela.

"I'm taking Ms. Casado to her room," the nurse says.

"I think we have to go," I say to Gabriela. "I will be back first thing in the morning. Get some rest and relax." I squeeze her hand again and she limply squeezes back.

Ingrid takes a moment to kiss her on the forehead and we leave together. As we walk down the hallway back to the waiting area, I find myself speechless. I can't help but think about what Gabriela had said.

I haven't been with anyone.

Either she's still groggy from surgery and the drugs, or something else is going on. Either way, I'm exhausted and I know that I need to get to sleep so that I can wake up and get back up here as soon as possible.

CHAPTER ELEVEN

Rett

I see Nico emerge from the patient recovery rooms and I stand from my seat. My ass is tingling from sitting for so long and the clock on the wall says we've been here for nearly five hours. I can hear, almost literally, my bed back home calling my name.

Nico walks up to me like she's shell-shocked. "Are you okay?" I ask. "You look like you've been through the war."

"I'm just…" she trails off.

I instinctively take her up in my arms and hold her. She breaks down and begins crying and I hold her tighter.

After a minute, she pulls away and swipes at her eyes, the mascara smearing as it does. She looks like a burglar or a racoon.

An incredibly adorable racoon, with gorgeous hazel

eyes that I want to get lost in.

The rest of the girls swarm Nico and she fills them in on the situation. They all start talking at once, unbelieving and in shock. I stand by Nico as she tells them that there's nothing else to do tonight and to go home.

Nico releases another sigh and turns to me. "I need to get some rest so I can get back up here in the morning. What time is it anyway?" She pulls her phone out of her purse and looks at the screen. "Jesus."

"Yeah," I say. "It's already morning."

"Well, I can get five-ish hours of sleep if I call an Uber right now," she says as she opens the device and starts swiping through apps.

I hold up a hand. "You don't need an Uber."

She looks at me dismissively. "Of course I do. How else will I get home? Walk?"

"No," I say confidently. "I had Clay leave my truck up here. Dave picked him up." I reach in my pocket and pull out my keys, dangling them in front of her. "I'll give you a ride."

She smiles, exhaustion on her face coupled with something that resembles relief. The fact that she doesn't have to ride in the back of some stranger's car at nearly four in the morning gives me a sense of relief too.

"You just think of everything, don't you?"

"I'd like to think that I have a handle on things, yeah." I nod toward the front door. "Come on, let's get out of here."

We make our way to the parking lot.

"Lot C," I say out loud.

"That way," Nico points.

After a few minutes of searching and me pushing the unlock button on the key fob, we see the tail lights flicker in response. Once in the pickup, Nico leans into the passenger seat as if she's trying to sink into it. I realize, as we pull out of the parking lot and onto the boulevard that will lead us back to the main highway, that she's silently sobbing. I reach over in front of her and open the glove compartment, pulling out a travel-sized container of tissues.

She accepts them with a slight smile and dabs at her eyes with one.

"You like to cry in pickups, it's cool," I say. "I prefer mine at the nail salon. I can really open up to the ladies."

Nico snorts. "I just don't understand," she finally says, her voice quivering. "But at the same time…"

"These things happen," I say. Probably not the most comforting thing in the moment and I even wince at my own words. "What I mean is, it's never always perfect. And, if anything, your friend is lucky to have you, have someone close who cares."

"Thank you. That's not what I mean, though," Nico says. "What I mean is, I don't know when she would have even had…"

"Had the opportunity to get pregnant?" I say.

"Right. Gabriela's not seeing anyone, at least not that I know of. And she certainly hasn't mentioned being with anyone."

"Wild night out recently?" I suggest. "I don't mean to insinuate that she's—"

"She's not a slut," Nico says defensively, her tired eyes boring holes in my face.

"I was going to say promiscuous, thank you," I retort.

"Oh."

"Yeah. Anyway, all I'm saying is, things happen, whether under the influence of alcohol or not, sometimes we don't even mean for them to. Despite all that, I think Gabriela's incredibly lucky to have someone like you in her life. I take it she doesn't have family nearby?"

"No, most of her family is still in Montana. I think her dad is in Ohio these days – Columbus maybe? – but they haven't spoken in a few years."

"I know what that's like. And I'm assuming you do, too. Being in a city away from any family. If anything happened to me, it would be Clay in your shoes."

"You guys seem really close," she says, her voice steady and no longer sobbing.

"We've been friends for a long time. He's one of the few guys I can go to with any problem. Like tonight. Dude is always there."

"Have you told him about your writer's block?" she asks.

I give her a sideways glance as I turn onto the access road that goes to the highway. "I haven't outright come out and said anything, but I know he knows. But that's Clay, man. He's supportive as hell. Without him, who knows where I'd be. Which reminds me—"

"Oh, take this exit," she says, pointing to the green sign on the right side of the road.

I drift over to the exit lane.

"Sorry," she said. "Remind you of what?"

"The notebook. The new journal you sent to my rehearsal space."

"I literally don't know what you're talking about," Nico says.

"Well, who else would send a notebook like that? It's really nice. Leather cover and everything."

"Maybe it's Clay," Nico shrugs. "But doesn't want you knowing that it's him."

That would be a possibility, except that he seemed just as surprised as everyone else that a package had been delivered to our musical fortress of solitude. Unless he's a better actor than he's ever been in our friendship, I scratch the idea.

She gives me a few more directions, and we're at the curb in front of her apartment building. Nico sits for a minute, unmoving.

"Thank you," she finally says. "For everything this evening. For just being there."

"I would like to think that if the situation was reversed, you'd do the same."

"Yeah. Maybe." She gives me her own sly smile.

"Goodnight," I say.

"Goodnight. Thanks again." She gets out of the truck and I watch as she walks up the steps of the building, disappearing into the stairwell that leads to the loft apartments above the ground floor. It's a lot like the building I live in, an old brick rectangle, restored amid the ongoing gentrification of downtown Nashville.

Just as I put the truck in drive, Nico comes crashing through those doors.

"Hey!" she cries out.

My heart immediately jumps out of my chest. I put the truck in park.

"What's wrong?" I ask as I get out.

"It's Monster," she says.

"What the hell is monster?" I ask, confused.

"He's our cat. Anyway, he's got himself stuck inside the couch again. Can you help me get him out?"

I sigh and follow Nico upstairs. On the landing, she opens the door to the apartment and I can immediately hear the cat hissing and clawing beneath the couch in the living area.

"There's a hole in the lining and he'll crawl up in there sometimes. Usually Gabriela is here to coax him out. I can't lift the couch by myself."

"What do you want me to do?" I ask.

"Just lift the couch and I'll see if I can pull him out," she says.

"He sounds pissed off," I say, as I follow her to the couch.

"You would be too if you were stuck under there. No telling how long he's been hissing and waiting for one of us to rescue him."

I take a position on the far end of the brown suede couch and crouch next to it. Looping my hands beneath the base, I nod at Nico. She nods back and I count to three. At three, I lift.

And a giant creature, all orange and claws, hissing and making demon noises, sprints out from under the couch and attacks my leg, scratching at my jeans. It digs its claws in and starts biting and settling those claws deep into my skin. It's all I can do to keep from dropping the couch on it.

"What the fuck is that?!" I exclaim to Nico, still holding onto the couch. "I thought you said it was a cat!"

"He is a cat!" Nico says. She comes to my side and swats at the animal with her foot. He finally takes off down the hallway to some unknown space, probably under a bed to wait for his next attack.

Finally, I drop the couch back onto the floor.

"Sorry about that," Nico says. "I should have warned you. Are you okay?"

I sit down on the couch and lift my pant leg where I've been attacked. There are red scratch marks on my shin and they are starting to sting.

"I don't know," I say. "You may have to amputate."

"I'll go grab a butter knife," Nico says. She then smacks my shin.

"Ow!" I yelp and rub it with my palm. "That was a jerk move."

"You'll be fine," Nico says. "Unless you're allergic to cats."

"I don't think I am. But also a question you probably should've asked before you led me into a deathtrap."

"Oh my god, I didn't think of every possible scenario," she sighs.

"Where did you even find that thing?" I ask. I turn again, checking my back to make sure he's not behind me, preparing a sneak attack.

"He just showed up one day," Nico says with a yawn. "Do you want me to get you some Tylenol? Some hydrogen peroxide?"

"Sure," I say.

Nico leaves me on the couch, and I lean back onto the cushion, its softness enveloping me. I close my eyes for a moment and wait for her to return with the pain medicine.

* * *

I open my eyes and immediately freak out. I don't know where I am. I'm in an apartment, but it's not mine. And I'm not in my own bed. I'm on a couch.

The previous night comes flooding back, including getting attacked by that demon that Nico claims is a cat. That's no cat. For one, cats don't get that big. Two, their eyes don't glow red.

I sit up and take in my surroundings. The early morning light is not doing me any favors. Judging from the lack of noise, I think I'm the only one awake. My boots are on the ground beside me, but I'm still in my jeans and flannel from last night. The living room is part of a large open space that includes the kitchen and a dining area. It's a complete mess. There are shoes of various sizes on the floor, and the dining table looks like it's more a clothes hamper than a place to eat.

I get up and make my way into the kitchen. There's a coffee maker on the counter, and after digging through some of the cabinets, I find a bag of grounds and a couple of mugs. I figure that if Nico's anything like me, she'll want coffee before she has to go back to the hospital.

I fill the carafe with water and dump it into the reservoir and fill the filter with coffee grounds. After a few moments, the machine gurgles to life and as coffee drips into the glass carafe, the smell of morning emanates through the kitchen and the entire apartment. The older I've gotten, the more my days require me to start with this stuff. At one time, I could get up, throw on a pair of jeans and a t-shirt and go. These days, I need time to let all my systems start up, and coffee is the fuel to jumpstart it all.

Looking around the kitchen for something to cook up for breakfast, my hunt is interrupted by Nico. She's in an oversized t-shirt and a pair of pajama pants, her hair a mess on top of her head. But good God she is so cute. She's standing in the doorway between the hallway that I assume leads to the bedrooms and the open living area.

"What are you doing?" she asks, seeming slightly perturbed.

"Sorry if I woke you," I say. "I was just making some coffee. Seeing if you have some bacon or something. I was going to cook you breakfast."

"No, you're getting out of here so I can get ready to head back to the hospital," she says matter-of-factly.

I point to the coffee maker. "I can have coffee first though, right?"

She sighs. "Yes."

"Good," I say. "Now come sit down, let me make you a cup. You had a long night."

"You have no idea," she says, looking away as she slides onto a barstool on the opposite side of the counter from me.

The coffee maker spurts as it finishes brewing and I pour up a mug for her. "Cream and sugar?"

"There's a bottle of cinnamon vanilla creamer in the fridge," she nods toward the stainless-steel refrigerator.

I grab the creamer and top off the mug for her.

"Thank you," she says, taking a sip.

I pour my own mug, sans creamer, and take a sip as well. "You're welcome."

"Straight black?" she says with a grimace.

"It'll do for today," I say.

"The only people who drink their coffee black are serial killers and my grandfather. Who, I'm pretty certain was a serial killer," she says.

"I'm no serial killer, but I'm sure I'd make a hot grandpa. A G-dilf," I say. I smile at my own joke, and she looks at me like I'm the lamest guy on the planet. "Oh come on," I argue. "I'm kidding. Why was your grandpa a suspected serial killer?"

"Because," she says, taking another sip, "he would work out in his garden in the middle of the summer in long-sleeve coveralls. Then, he'd come inside for his breakfast, which consisted of black coffee and toast with tabasco sauce."

"Whoa," I say, impressed. "That's not a serial killer. That's a badass. Let me guess – he was a military guy."

"Army. Korea," she says.

"My grandpa was the same way. No tabasco and toast, but the same thing. Black coffee, rolled his own cigarettes. Something those guys went through in their youth carved a line of toughness in their brains. It carried them through their lives," I say.

"That's," she says, pausing. "Really poetic."

"I'm not out of ideas. I just can't get them to come out as lyrics," I say. I look down at the mug on the counter in front of me, seeing my own reflection in the inky liquid. Even there, I can see dark circles under my eyes. I look rough.

Nico, on the other hand, looks amazing. Flawless. Sitting there, drinking her coffee. She should be like a zombie, but she's just…perfect.

She breaks me out of my concentration. "I need you to leave," she says.

I look at her, puzzled. "What, now?" I say.

"Yes. Now."

"Oh," I start. "Okay. Just let me get my boots."

I finish my coffee and put the mug in the sink. She doesn't say another word as I get my boots on. She doesn't even look at me.

"Thanks for letting me crash on your couch," I say.

No response.

I sigh, and walk out the front door and into the cold morning air, wondering what I said or did to make her change so dramatically.

CHAPTER TWELVE

Nico

I feel bad for making him leave like that, but I just couldn't be alone with him anymore. I tried to push my anxiety down below the surface, but it wouldn't go away.

Even last night, when he fell asleep on my couch, I thought about waking him up and making him leave right then. But he'd given me a ride home and hadn't even given me any reason to think he would try something.

To be safe, I slept with my door locked, and the baseball bat resting against my nightstand.

I haven't been alone with a guy in a long time. It's nothing Rett did or said, but I just couldn't keep it bottled in any longer. I couldn't even look at him as he left, softly shutting the front door behind him.

I push it all away and focus on what needs to happen right now. I need to shower and get to the hospital. A list of tasks to mark off my mental to-do list, I start on them immediately.

Switching the coffee maker off, I quickly wash both of our mugs. I can't help but hold the one Rett drank out of. He's so handsome. And sweet. Standing there in my kitchen, leaning against the counter, I could get used to seeing that every morning. For a split second, I let myself imagine what it would be like. To wake up to him every day, to work together, to write, to see him in his element.

But it's not something I can allow myself to do. I can't get involved with anyone again.

And still…

I push that away too, and I put the mug away in the cabinet. Ticking off boxes, staying on task.

In less than an hour, I'm showered, dressed and waiting for an Uber to take me to the hospital. My stomach is growling, and I realize that the only thing I've had to eat were the snacks that Rett bought from the vending machine in the emergency room's waiting area. I need actual food, another task on my mental to-do list.

The Uber pulls up, a silver Jeep Grand Cherokee, and I hop into the backseat. The driver, an older woman, turns down the radio to verify my destination. She's listening to a church service.

"Metro General, yes ma'am," I say.

She nods and smiles at me through the rearview mirror and starts toward the hospital. The drive is mostly silent on both our parts. The only time she says anything to me – and vice-versa – is when she tells me to have a good day.

I do my best to smile, but already my stomach is in knots as I walk up to the front entrance of the hospital. The lobby and entryway are massive, with high ceilings and an escalator that leads to a second floor, where the smells from the buffet-style cafeteria emanate down here. My stomach growls again, in protest of the lack of nutrients I've put in it in the last twelve-ish hours.

The elevator ride to the floor where they've taken Gabriela is long and slow.

Finally, I come to her room, and knock on the door as I make my way in.

"Hey sweetie," I say as I enter the dimly lit room. She's awake, sitting up in the hospital bed, the standard green gown covered with white sheets.

"Hi," she says with a forced smile.

I find a chair and pull it up next to her bed and take her hand in mine. "How're you feeling?"

"Like I've been hit by my dad's combine tractor," she says, stifling a laugh.

I can't help but crack a smile as well. "Do you remember that time we threw that party in the field sophomore year?"

"Yes," she laughs. "He found beer bottles in that pasture for six months and every time he did, he threatened to ground me all over again."

"I miss those days, Gab," I sigh.

"I do too," she says. Her response is sad. Longing, even. Longing for a past that we both gave up, a simple life that we traded in for whatever it was that we decided to chase.

For her, it was the fashion industry. For me, the notoriety that my words brought me.

I didn't know it would bring me everything else too.

And I doubt she thought that her path would lead her to this hospital room.

As if she can read my mind – and perhaps it was just written on my face – she looks away from me, turning her eyes to the curtained window that looks out to the parking lot eight stories below. "I know what you're thinking," she says softly.

"It's okay," I say. "I just wish you would have told me you were seeing someone."

"I'm not," she says. "I didn't want you to think less of me."

"Nothing could make me think less of you," I reassure her.

"It was almost two months ago, before one of the shows. You know, the one for Virgin? I went to the afterparty and had too much to drink. I woke up the next morning…" she breaks off, tears in her eyes.

"It's okay, Gab," I say. "It happens."

"But it shouldn't have." She's sobbing now, and I grab a tissue from a box on the side of the hospital bed. Gabriela dabs at her eyes with it. "I'm so ashamed."

"There's nothing to be ashamed of," I comfort her, caressing her free hand. The other is still attached to the IV, the bag connected to the metal stand dripping lazily.

"I should've been more careful. I should've listened to the other girls. They told me he was dangerous."

My eyebrows raise immediately out of concern. "What are you talking about? Who is dangerous?"

After a few heartbeats of silence, she sighs. Without looking at me, she simply says, "It was Max."

My heart catches in my throat for a moment. Max?

"Does he know?" was the only thing that could come out of my lips, completely blindsided by the revelation.

"I don't think so. I didn't even know myself, you know," she says, which, given her current situation, I should've thought about before the question even escaped my mouth.

"I mean, are you going to tell him?"

"What's the point?" Her eyes turn away, and I can't tell if it's shame or something else. "I mean, there's no baby to even tell him about."

"But still," I argue. "He's your boss."

"I know that, Nicole."

"He took advantage of you." My heart is beating irregularly now, and my palms are sweaty.

"No he didn't," she says, turning back to me. "It was my choice."

"Despite whether it was your choice or not, he's your superior, and he used that as leverage to sleep with you. There's no telling how many other girls he's done that to."

"It doesn't matter," she says haughtily. Obviously,

she's thought about it as well, whether she wants to discuss it or not.

I'm still in disbelief, more so that she would put herself in that kind of situation with Max Van Hope.

The Van Hopes have essentially run the entertainment industry in Nashville – and the greater south, for all intents and purposes – for over fifty years. Max and his sister Laura inherited their respective positions after the elder Van Hope died from a heart attack nearly a decade ago.

Whereas Laura Van Hope manages her record label, keeps her business straight as an arrow, and runs a tight ship, her younger brother has found himself on the front page of tabloids several times over. A better choice would've been to have Laura Van Hope run everything, whether she wanted the responsibility or not. She would've been a much better choice to run a fashion empire than Max. If anything, they were in the wrong positions, and everyone knew it.

I put aside all these thoughts and take Gabriela's hand. "I'm here for you, and in a few hours we can get you home to rest and relax."

She looks up at me. "Thank you."

"In the meantime, I am absolutely starving," I say.

She cracks a grin. "Want some leftover Jello?" She nods to an empty bowl that still contains flecks of green gelatin.

I laugh. "No thanks. I'm going to head down to the cafeteria though. Whatever they have cooking smells amazing. I'll probably order one of everything." I lean over and kiss Gabriela on the forehead. "I'll be right back."

"I'm not going anywhere," she says with a smile.

There's my girl. She'll get through this.

Though, as I walk toward the cafeteria, all I can think about is taking down Max Van Hope.

* * *

"Here you are," Rett says as he pulls his truck up to the curb to our apartment building. Putting the truck in park, he gets out and opens the passenger door for Gabriela, helping her onto the sidewalk.

I get out of the backseat, and, taking her arm, assist her in walking up the steps to the building. Rett follows behind us, carrying bags slung over his shoulders. He's got them crossed like bandoliers and I can't help but laugh at how ridiculous, and cute, he looks.

When Gabriela was being released, he was the only person I could think of that could come pick her up and take us back to the apartment. Sometimes living in the city without a vehicle is okay. It's almost perfectly feasible to live on Uber to get around. However, emergencies have proven that it can also be a hassle.

He came right away, too, dropping whatever he was up to. In the car, he had some music on, and I could tell immediately that it was a demo from his band. The instrumentation was unpolished, but not rough, and he hummed a melody over the chorus. I liked seeing that he was working, putting some effort into the songwriting. The words would come, I'm sure. He just needs to get out of his head.

We make it to the front door, and I swing it open. Together, Rett and I help Gabriela in, and he deposits the bags by the door. I take Gabriela to her bedroom and help her onto the bed.

"What can I get you?" I ask as we take off her sweat-pants and t-shirt and change her into an extra-large shirt from her pajama drawer.

"Just a bottle of water for now," she says.

"I'll have to see if we have any," I say. I should've thought about getting some things for the apartment. Food, water, stuff for a few days.

I go to the kitchen and look in the fridge. There's one bottle of water left, and I sigh in relief. "I'm going to have to make a grocery run," I say, more to myself than to Rett, who's sitting at the bar, scrolling on his phone.

"I've already taken care of it," he says.

"What?"

"The groceries," he says. "I've already got them or-dered. Amazon will deliver before four today."

I am stunned. "Are you serious?"

"Of course," he shrugs. "I saw your fridge this morn-ing, it's clear you weren't in any position to play nurse for more than two hours. I got Jello, soups, Gatorade, stuff like that. Easy on her stomach as she recovers."

"Wow," I say, slightly stunned at how much he'd

thought of. "Um, thank you."

"You're welcome," he says with a smile.

I take the bottle of water to Gabriela and place it on her nightstand. She's already falling back asleep, so I pull the blankets over her shoulders and turn off the lamp on her bedside table.

Back in the kitchen, I start the coffee maker. "I could use an afternoon pick-me-up," I say.

"Same," Rett says. "You wouldn't believe how awful I feel. Like I slept on a couch all night." He smirks.

"You poor thing," I give him a fake pouty look. "I could've just kicked you out at five in the morning."

"I may have preferred it," he says. "Then I would've been able to sleep in instead of scrounging around your apartment at ten looking for coffee and food."

"In all seriousness, I'm sorry you didn't sleep well, but I'm glad you were here," I say. The coffee maker behind me spurts as it finishes brewing and I pour two mugs. I slide one over to him. "Thank you for everything."

"It's no problem," he says, and gives me that charming, gorgeous smile again. The one that I can't stop thinking about. I'm convinced that he's not only the most gorgeous man alive, but also the kindest. The way he's dropped everything to help Gabriela and me, I can't help but be slightly infatuated with him.

"Hey, I've got something to show you," he says as he takes a sip. From his back pocket, Rett produces a notebook. He opens it up from the ribbon bookmark, splays it out, and turns it toward me. I look down. It's words.

Lyrics. They tell the story of men returning from a war, finding their true loves waiting for them. It reminds me of our conversation this morning about our grandfathers, their similarities.

"After we talked this morning, when I went home, I wrote this. What do you think?"

I think it's amazing. It's obviously a first draft, his handwriting scrawled, with words scratched out, more writing in the gutter of the page, things circled and starred. But the story of the lyrics is exactly the kind of song that the record label is wanting from Rett Gordon and The Last Train Home.

"I'm proud of you," I say. "It's really, really good."

"The chorus," he says, "is what I was humming in the car. Clay wrote the music, and I kind of matched this to it."

"I think you've got something here," I say. "It's definitely a start, a place to build from." I take the notebook in my hands. It's beautiful leather, with his initials embossed on the front cover. "Is this the mysterious notebook?"

"Yeah," he says. "Maybe it's magical, because it's already working." He gives me a sideways glance, a little smirk across his lips. "You're sure you didn't send this?"

I huff. "Yes, I'm sure." Its leather cover is pretentious, even for my standards. I generally use cheap notebooks for my writing. I've never been one to splurge on something that I'm just going to scribble all over. I read his lyrics again. "Do you mind if I make some notes?"

Rett shrugs and sips his coffee. "Go ahead. We're supposed to be doing this together after all."

I rummage in one of the drawers in the kitchen and find a gel pen in one under the microwave on the counter. With the notebook, I slide into the bar-height chair at the counter next to Rett.

I read the lyrics and circle some of the more descriptive words, focusing on the theme and the ways we can call back from the first verse to the final verse.

"So, this is from the perspective of coming back from a war, so we should use more peaceful wording toward the end, to show that progression," I say. "As he's back home and with his love, those horrors are further and further behind."

Rett nods in agreement. "I like that. It's like a story, you know? I guess all music is that way. The song tells a story."

"Right," I say, making notes in his notebook. As he discusses the song and the emotions he's trying to convey with it, I write down some more of his thoughts, letting him talk in a stream-of-conscious style while I jot down some of the more poignant aspects.

Now that I've got it in my hands, the notebook is incredibly nice, with smooth, high-quality paper. It's like something from one of the more expensive stationery shops, not a mass-produced black rectangle available at any big-box bookstore. No, this was meticulously crafted. It's well-made and worth the words we are pouring into it.

"So," I say, "just building upon some of your thoughts, the song takes on more of a cathartic feeling. Toward the end, when the narrator is looking back on his life, and the woman that was there through it all, we can really feel how much he loves her and how much she's saved him."

He leans down and reads some of my notes, the words in the gutters of the pages and some extra lines. "It's perfect," he says, looking up at me.

Those gorgeous green eyes stare right into my soul, and it makes heat jolt through my body. I can't help but linger on them, letting that feeling radiate through me. After a few moments, I finally pull my eyes from his gaze.

"Well, not perfect yet," I say. "But it's a fantastic start. If you record a demo of this and turn it in to Giant, I know they'll love it. But our job is to write hits, to write songs that will stick. So, we need a bit more time with it."

"You're really good at this," he says. "Thank you for your help." He looks down at his feet, his shoulders slump. "I'm sorry for how I treated you when we first met. It's not your fault that I felt slighted by the label."

I give him a warm smile. "It's okay. It's completely understandable, but I'm glad you've come around. I think we've got some good work in us."

Again, he flashes that smile and again I want to melt into him. But that's what got me in trouble before, so I make myself pull my infatuation back. I down my coffee.

His phone dings and he pulls it out of his back pocket.

"Ah," he says. "The grocery delivery has arrived." Getting up from the table, he walks to the front door just as the delivery person knocks to announce their arrival. It gives me a few moments to collect myself. I remind myself that we are working together.

Rett brings the bags inside and deposits them on the counter top. Organizing them, he puts things – bottles of water, packages of Jello, cans of soup – away in counters and the fridge.

"This is really nice of you," I finally say, as he folds up the plastic sacks.

My stomach growls and I look at the clock on my phone. It's just after seven, and I realize the only thing I've had to eat all day is a sausage biscuit from the hospital's cafeteria.

"Hey," I say. "I know you just bought all this food, but would you like some takeout? I'm starving."

He nods. "Yeah, absolutely. I can always eat." He points to the plastic sacks that he's been folding. "I save these for trash bags. Do you want me to put them away or into recycling?"

"They go in that cabinet over there." I point to a cabinet beneath the sink.

Rett opens it and a pile of wadded-up sacks threaten to spill out.

"Why didn't you tell me you just threw them in here like a heathen? I spent all this time making them nice and uniform," he sighs emphatically.

I can't help but laugh. "Let me check on Gabriela real

quick and then we can go grab some dinner. There's a really good Asian place a few blocks down, and I could go for some beef jerky and sticky rice."

He stands up from the cabinet. "You know about beef jerky and sticky rice?"

"Uh," I say. "Yeah. It's the best stuff ever."

"Say no more. I'm one hundred percent down for this place. I haven't had good beef jerky and sticky rice in for-ever."

"Well, Sushi House makes the best," I say. "I'll be right back."

Cracking the door to Gabriela's room, I can tell she's sleeping hard. I tip-toe over to her bed and gently nudge her. "Hey sweetie. Do you need anything?"

She grumbles a no.

"I'm going to Sushi House with Rett. I'll be back in thirty minutes."

"Okay," she mumbles, though I doubt she's con-scious enough to really understand what's going on.

It's times like these that I wish we had family closer. It would be nice to have our mothers here – they both would do a much better job at the nursing thing than I am. As I shut her door, I take one more glance at her in the dark, her long body curled up beneath the duvet. I hate seeing her like this, but even more, I hate that I could have done something about it sooner.

I take a deep breath before I emerge back into the light of the open living area.

"Ready?" I ask.

"Absolutely," Rett says.

Together, we walk down the sidewalk toward Sushi House. I explain to him how, when I first moved to Nashville, I would walk all over the neighborhood, exploring and getting used to my new home, my new surroundings.

"What brought you here?" he asks. "Why Nashville? I know you didn't come to write country music."

"I just needed to get out of Texas," I say, which isn't untrue. But for several reasons – many I'm not willing to talk about.

"Right, but you could have gone anywhere. You're from Montana, right? Why not go back there?"

"Because I couldn't go back home," I say. I feel myself tensing, and Rett stops on the sidewalk to turn to me.

"Look, I don't want this to devolve into whatever happened this morning. I like you. I like working with you. And if I approach a subject you don't want to talk about, you can just tell me. It's okay."

I allow myself to relax. "You're right," I say. "And I'm sorry for this morning. It's just...so much is going on right now, and I haven't quite been able to wrap my brain around it all." I don't tell him that Gabriela's situation brought up some feelings and anxieties that I thought were dormant.

"Tell me about it," Rett says. He falls back in lockstep with me as we turn the corner and cross the street. Sushi House, with its lit neon sign, is just a few blocks ahead now. "But I feel good about the album now."

"Good. I do too," I say with a smile.

"I do have one question though," he says apprehensively. "Your roommate's friends, they all call you Nicole. Is that your real name?"

I nod slowly. "Yeah."

"So Nico is just…" he trails off.

"A pseudonym."

"Cool. I like it."

"My real name is Nicole Johnson." It's a name I haven't called myself in a long time, not since college. It sounds foreign to me now, despite Gabriela still calling me Nicole.

"I'm just Everett Gordon," he says. "There were too many syllables for the band name, so I shortened it to Rett."

"Have you always gone by Rett?" I ask.

"I've actually never gone by Rett. But that's what everyone calls me now. I just had to get used to it. What do you prefer me to call you?"

"You can call me Nicole. I feel like myself around you," I say, realizing how comfortable I am with him before the words even leave my mouth.

He smiles. "Okay, Nicole."

We get to the restaurant and order, carrying our dinner back to my apartment.

I put *Schitt's Creek* on and we eat, talking and laughing. Despite everything that's going on right now, it feels good to relax, and it feels good to be with Rett.

CHAPTER THIRTEEN

Rett

For the second morning in a row, I wake up on Nico's – Nicole's – couch. Except this time, she's tucked up under my arm, her body stretched out, her feet hanging off the end of the opposite armrest. I resist moving in fear of waking her up and startling her. I can't help but admire how peaceful and beautiful she is.

Still, there's something below the surface that she keeps to herself, locked away, and it keeps her from being completely open and comfortable.

Last night was a change of pace though. We laughed and hung out, and watched too many episodes of Schitt's Creek before eventually passing out. Our takeout containers are still on the coffee table in front of us, and the television is on, but the screen is black.

I blink myself awake and Nicole stirs in my arms. She

yawns and looks up at me, at first with a sweet smile before she bolts up.

"Oh my god," she says. "What time is it?"

I find my phone in my pocket. "Just after seven," I say. My battery is close to dying, the battery indicator in the top right-hand corner is red.

"I need to check on Gabriela," she says. She stands up and almost sprints down the hall.

After a minute, she comes back.

"She's zonked out," she says.

"She probably will be for another day or so," I say. I stretch and yawn.

"I should probably head out," I add, gathering the garbage from the night before. "Thank you for letting me crash here... again."

"Yeah, yeah," she says, leaning in the doorway. "I may have to charge you rent if you keep this up."

I laugh and toss the boxes into the trash bag in the kitchen. "Send the bill to the label. Consider it a business expense."

"That would go over real well," she snorts.

This is the second morning in a row I've woken up to Nicole and I still swear she's more beautiful in the morning than most women are in an entire lifetime.

"What are you staring at?" she asks coyly.

"Just, thinking about last night," I say, as I shove our garbage from dinner into her trash can beside the fridge. "I'm not going to pretend I don't see it. You have a past that you're trying to leave behind. And I get that. But I just want you to know you can be yourself with me."

She looks away for a moment before meeting my gaze. That coy smile is gone, replaced with something else. Resolve, maybe?

"Thank you," she says.

"I hate to leave you alone, but I've got to get out of here," I say. I'm still in my clothes from all day yesterday, and want a shower, and to sleep in my own bed for a night. Plus, I've got to get my guitar and gear from Clay's place. He was kind enough to grab it from the venue the other night, and I haven't seen him since.

"I'm not going to lie," she says. "But I need a shower."

"I was thinking the same thing," I say.

Nicole's eyebrows raise.

"Me," I clarify, averting my eyes. "Myself. I also need a shower."

"Come here," she says, with her arms outstretched.

I walk over to her and envelope her in my own embrace, feeling her body sink into mine, her head on my chest. I could stay right here for the rest of the day if she asked me to. Maybe even longer. The shower can wait.

"Thank you," she says without lifting her head from my chest.

I just hold her, right here in the doorway between the hall and the living area.

She continues, "For everything. I couldn't have gotten through these past two days without your help."

"I'm happy to," I say, my chin on the crown of her head. She smells good, like coconut and lavender. "And if you need anything else, I'm a phone call away."

"Phone call?" she asks with fake concern. "Who still calls?"

"Old people, like me," I say.

I don't know where it comes from, but I lean my head down and kiss the top of her head, taking in the scent of her.

She snuggles me harder and then lifts her eyes up to me. I don't know how it happens – something about magnets, probably – but my lips are drawn to hers. My entire body shudders with excited nervousness. With one hand pressed to the small of her back, I reach the other to cup her cheek and pull her lips to mine.

Her tongue parts my lips as she pulls herself closer into me. Her mouth is soft and full. I pick her up, feel her legs wrap around my waist and I press her against the wall, her arms wrap around me greedily. She arches her neck and I kiss my way down her jawline. She tastes incredible and I can't get enough.

With my face cradled in her hands, she pulls my lips back to hers. It's a moment that stretches for eternity, but feels much too short.

"Okay," she pants, pulling her lips away. "We have to stop."

"You're right," I say, though it's the last thing I want to do. I want to keep kissing her, keep feeling her hands on my face, feeling them explore my back and my chest, her body heat radiating into me.

I let her down back onto her own two feet and she

keeps her hands on my chest. Her lip and neck are splotchy red from the stubble of my beard.

"Goodness," she says. "That was…"

"Yeah," I say. "Yeah it was."

"Came out of nowhere."

"Yeah."

"Thank you," Nicole says again. "For all your help, not just…not just that. I'll call you."

"You better. We still have an entire album to write."

She laughs and lets go of my embrace. I make sure I have my phone and wallet before walking out the door, getting one more glimpse of her standing there in her living room. I can't wait to see her again.

* * *

"You look like shit," Clay says with a laugh.

"Well, I've slept on a couch for two nights straight and my back is feeling it. I'm too damn young for my back to hurt like this."

Clay laughs again and digs in the cabinet above the kitchen sink and finds a bottle of Advil. He tosses it over my way and I catch it with a slight juggle.

"So that's it?" he asks. "You just slept on her couch?"

"That's it. We had a good time though. She took me to this awesome sushi place last night. We got carryout and took it back to her apartment and watched some Netflix," I say. I pop open the medicine bottle and jam a couple of capsules in my mouth, chasing them with a swig from the bottle of room temperature water in front of me.

"Ah," he says, rocking his eyebrows. "A little Netflix and chill?"

"No, no," I say, but I feel my cheeks go red. "None of that. We're working together, man."

"That's how it always starts in those books, you know. Forced to work together, and then the next thing you know, they're in the sheets as the female lead character goes on and on about all the orgasms the handsome new-comer gives her."

I stare at him with actual concern. "Clay. What the fuck kind of books are you reading?"

"Good ones. You have to know the inner psyche of women. And romance novels are the best way to do that."

I hold up a hand. "I don't want to know any more."

"Nonetheless, that sounds like where it's heading," he says.

"It's not," I retort, taking another swig from the water bottle. "Now let's go get my guitars."

Clay leads me down his hallway to his studio room. His apartment is a two bedroom and he's converted the second bedroom at the end of the hall into a demo re-cording room. There's an iMac on a desk surrounded by MIDI controllers, mixers, and studio monitors. A bass sits on a stand in the corner and instrument cables litter the floor. This is where he demoes song ideas and records them for the rest of us. Of the four band members, he is the most technical, the most talented when it comes to music composition. If this band were to not work out, or after we hang it up, I imagine that he's going to be a famous and sought-after music producer.

In the corner of the room, my guitar case is on the ground. "Dave took the amplifiers. He was going back to the rehearsal space anyway, so he decided to take all the heavy equipment."

"Good," I say, relieved. "I wasn't exactly looking forward to carrying it all back down three flights of stairs."

"Yeah. He wanted to schedule another rehearsal too. Before the next show."

"Absolutely. We need to go over that new breakdown a couple of times to tighten it up," I say. I open the tweed case and check my guitar. I have no doubts that it was well taken care of in my absence, but I just want to look at it. My baby, this instrument has been with me through it all, and sometimes I simply just admire it. I feel my new notebook sticking out my back pocket as I squat, and I pull it out.

"Oh," I say. "Check this out. Nicole and I worked on this."

Clay takes the book from my hands and flips it open to the ribbon bookmark.

"I like this," he nods. "I like it a lot."

"It just came out yesterday morning, and then Nicole and I workshopped it yesterday evening after I picked her and her roommate up from the hospital.

"Let's lay down a vocal track," Clay says, gesturing toward the computer. "We can get a demo down and have it ready for rehearsal."

I'm hesitant at first, but capitulate. It's not like I am doing anything today, and if nothing else, it will keep my mind off Nicole's lips. "Let's do it."

After a few retakes, we finally get the vocal track laid down over the demo recording we made of the song, and it's actually better than I could've even imagined. As Clay replays it through the monitors, I hold my phone up to record a snippet and send it to Nicole.

She responds almost immediately.

It sounds amazing!

I know! Thank you for all your help.

Just doing my job ;)

I am caught off guard by the flirtatious emoji. I decide to be flirtatious as well.

Wish I was your job ;)

OMG. Stop.

I can't help but think about that kiss in her living

room, feeling her body pressed against mine as I lifted her up and she wrapped her legs around my waist. It was so sudden yet so perfect, and all I want is to go back over to her apartment to make it happen again.

Clay brings me out of my own head. "Hey," he says. "Ground control to Major Tom. Did you hear me?"

"What?" I instinctively say, unaware that he'd been talking for the last few minutes.

"I said, what if we start the song with the chorus chords before going into the verse? It will pack a punch immediately and grab the listener right off the bat," he says.

"Oh. Yeah. Let's try that," I say.

As he sits in front of the giant computer monitor, he moves some tracks around in the recording program, dragging and dropping entire sections, cutting and splitting. It's amazing. This wouldn't have been possible even a few years ago. When I was a kid, I had a four-track unit that recorded to tape. There was no splicing, no cutting, no digital tools. But now with Pro Tools, it's much easier to manipulate the recordings to do whatever you want.

I watch in amazement as Clay finishes up with the new arrangement. He hits play and the metronome track starts. He raps his knuckles on the desk surface in time with the beat.

"That sounds pretty damn perfect," he says.

I agree. It's great hearing the first song completed, ready for submission to the label.

"Now just twenty more," I sigh. As good as it feels to

have this one written, I know that it's only about five percent of what needs to go into the full record. We still have to re-record the songs in our apartment-turned-recording-studio, and then have those recordings professionally mastered. Still, having one done feels like a major accomplishment.

"We'll get them," he says. "The good news is we've got the instrumentation written for most of the record. We just need to put it all together."

I nod in agreement, thankful for Clay's positive outlook on things.

"When are you and Nico getting together again?" he asks.

I stammer for an answer, my brain going completely blank. All I can think about is her body and her lips.

"You know, to write some more songs?" he clarifies.

"Oh, hopefully in the next week-ish," I say, gathering my thoughts. "She's going through a lot at the moment, and I plan on giving her a few days to get it all situated."

"Yeah, that's true," Clay says. "Maybe next time you see her, you'll be sure to wipe her lipstick off your neck after you do."

My eyes go wide and Clay bursts into laughter. I pull out my phone and, with the selfie camera, examine a clear pair of lips in pink lipstick planted squarely on my jawline. I wipe at them with my hand, smearing the color onto my palm. Clay just continues laughing.

CHAPTER FOURTEEN

Nico

In the last three weeks since Rett was here in my apartment, I've not gone one day without looking at that doorway where he lifted me off my feet and kissed me. I've never been kissed like that. Sure, I've been swept off my feet and I've had a few passionate romps, but nothing like that. It felt both electric and safe, like he wanted to ravage me and protect me.

I didn't think I'd allow myself to be kissed like that. Unfortunately, we haven't been able to recreate it. Or, perhaps, it's most fortunate. I feel like that if we get started like that again, it won't stop until I've got him in my bed.

Gabriela has physically healed from her emergency surgery. She still looks like a ghost, emotionless and distant. I do my best to be a shoulder to lean on, but I'm still adamant that she talks to someone about Max Van Hope. He can't be allowed to take advantage of these girls like that. I want her to reach out, to ask the other girls, but she's afraid that she'll be ostracized, perhaps even released from her contract.

When we're not working together, which usually happens at the coffee shop where I was scoping him out, Rett and I have been texting almost nonstop. He'll send me lyric ideas, little lines, through text. He'll send me a picture of his notebook, the scrawled letters sometimes legible, sometimes not. I don't care if I can read every word. The fact that he's producing ideas and sharing them with me is exactly what we need to get to the finish line. I've taken some of the lyrics and tweaked them as well, hoping that when they are polished, we'll have several songs ready to demo. The label wants six demoes by the end of next month, and I feel the crunch.

Clay e-mailed me a folder of all their current songs without lyrics. They've got about a dozen written. Rett and I will get the words written for them.

The band has another concert lined up this weekend at one of the country bars downtown, and I'm already giddy for it.

Actually, certifiably giddy.

I can't wait to see Rett back onstage again, the feeling of the drums and bass in my chest, and the sound of his voice. I even sometimes hear it in my dreams, the good ones.

Gabriela comes out of the bathroom and into the

kitchen where I'm preparing a week's worth of juice for smoothies. She nearly walks into the counter, her eyes glued to her phone in her hands.

"I cannot believe this," she says.

"What's going on?" I ask, suddenly seeing the despair and lack of color in her face.

"I've been left out of the next show," she says.

A bag of frozen bananas and strawberries slips out of my hands, the contents spilling on the counter surface. "What?" I ask. "Why?" I begin gathering up the red and yellow fruit, but I'm so flustered that they slip through my fingers, leaving my hands stained and sticky.

"Well, it doesn't say why, but I think we know." Gabriela takes a seat at the bar in front of me and I finally get all the fruit back in the bag.

"Well, how did you find out? An email or something?"

"Yeah," she says, her face still glued to the device in her hands. The plus-size iPhone would look enormous in my hands but fits just fine in her lanky fingers. "They've released the roster for the next show and I'm not on it."

"Well," I say, taking a moment to compose myself, "maybe they're giving you some extended time off to recover."

"No," she says, shaking her head. "I feel like I'm being shoved out now, without being explicitly told so. And what's worse is they know I need the money. They know I missed the last one because of the surgery, and now I'm being left off the itinerary."

"Is there someone you can talk to?" I ask. "Someone

besides…"

"No," she says, catching my question. "Max sets the schedule. Max does it all. The only person I have to be mad at is myself. I should've never slept with him."

"No, that's horseshit and you know it, Gab," I say. "He took advantage of you. He took advantage of his position. When are you going to confront them about that?"

"I can't, Nicole. It was consensual," she argues, but I hold my hands up.

"You can't actually believe that. What, actually, is consensual about someone in superior authority having sex with an employee?"

"I know what you're getting at, Nicole. If it were any other industry, I may have a shot. But I don't. There are a million girls in line behind me that want what I have, and it looks like they're going to get it." Gabriela slumps in the barstool, her body curving against the back of the chair.

I know I'm probably overstepping my boundaries, but after what happened in Texas, I never want to see another woman in this position, and yet here we are. I feel absolutely powerless to do anything about it.

"So what do you want to do?" I ask, folding my arms defiantly.

"I don't know yet. There are some other firms in town. I could probably get picked up by a production company doing commercials or something."

"And then what?" I say. "When word gets around and Max Van Hope has his dirty fingers in every crevice of every business you find yourself in?" I know I'm being harsh, but the sting of my own experience is rearing its ugly head.

"I don't know!" she exclaims, tears in her eyes. She hops up from the barstool, storming off down the hallway. I want to chase after her, to apologize, but I can't. I can't stand this, and I find myself wanting no part of it.

Besides, I'm under contract with the Van Hopes too. One wrong move and I, too, could be out of a job.

Instead, I grab my phone and text Rett.

You guys doing rehearsals today?

He responds almost immediately.

Yup.

Good. What's the address?
I want to come listen.

After he sends me the address, I hail an Uber and leave the apartment without saying goodbye. Maybe some loud music will help clear my head, or at the very least, drown out all these unwanted thoughts.

* * *

The Uber drops me off at the address Rett gave me. It looks like a nondescript warehouse with a couple of retail shops on the bottom floor. I would never expect that this faded brick building would house a country band's rehearsal pad, except I can hear the bass drum from the street through an open window. Between two of the retail shops, a narrow door leads to a staircase up to the building's second floor. Upstairs, there are four doors in a short hallway, but only one of them looks like it leads to a room that would be occupied by a band.

I don't bother knocking – I doubt they'd even hear it. Instead, I just walk in and I'm greeted by a scene that I wasn't expecting.

This loft has been completely transformed into a recording and rehearsal space. Where a living area should be, there's a makeshift stage with a drum riser. The kitchen is intact, but instead of a dining table, there's a foosball table and a dart board on the opposite wall. Neon beer signs decorate the wall that aren't covered in sound-dampening panels and a Middle Tennessee University flag is tacked up behind the drums. It looks like a dream bachelor pad for four guys in a country-rock band.

The guys are playing something that sounds vaguely familiar. Then it hits me. It's the first song that Rett and I wrote together. Everything in my body goes tingly, feeling it race up my spine, this shot of endorphins. It's like a high. And the best part is, the song sounds amazing live. Even better than the phone recording snippet that Rett sent me. I can already hear it in front of a cheering crowd. Or on the radio. I am simply in shock. *We* wrote this.

They see me come in and stop playing. Rett pulls his

earplugs and lets them hang around his neck.

"Hey!" he says, excited to see me. I match his enthusiasm with a wide grin of my own. "You got here quick!"

"Yeah, it's actually not far from my apartment. A mile or so. I could probably walk it if I felt like it."

"I wasn't going to say anything. I didn't want to seem like a stalker. *Hey, I could walk to your apartment from our rehearsal space whenever I'd like* doesn't seem like it puts off good boy vibes."

I laugh and pat his chest with my hand.

"Grab a beer, come hang out," he says. "You remember all the guys." He leaves me for the kitchen.

Clay comes over and fist bumps me. The other two guys politely nod.

"How's your roommate?" he asks.

"She's having a rough day, actually. Which is why I'm here. I needed to get out of the apartment for a bit."

"I get that," he says.

Rett returns with two beers. He cracks the cap of one and hands it to me.

I take the bottle from him. It's not Shiner, my usual beer of choice, but it's cold and perfect. It's warm outside, nearly unseasonably so, and I can tell that's why they have the windows open. The beer coats my throat and the alcohol is already loosening my wound-up nerves.

"What do you think?" Rett asks, gesturing to the loft apartment.

"This is great," I say, and I mean it. It looks like they've put a lot of work into this space. It looks like a safe space. "Do you guys pay for this, or does Giant Records?"

"Giant pays for the lease, but it was taken out of our initial signing bonus. Which is fine. We've made enough from live shows and merch that we could take a little less up front," Rett says.

"This is where we're going to record the next record," Clay says, popping the top of a beer himself. "We just need to finish the bathroom," he says.

I look at Rett quizzically.

"We're converting the bathroom's closet into a vocal booth," he says.

"Which seemed like a good idea until we realized how much Dave has to piss because of all his green juice," Clay laughs.

Dave's head perks up from his guitar amplifier that he'd been noodling with. "Hey," he calls out. "I can't help that I'm well-hydrated and healthy."

Rett laughs and shakes his head. "Anyway, yeah, this is our little oasis."

"I love it," I say.

"We were just playing through that song we wrote. Wanna hear it from the top?"

I smile. "Yes, please. I want to hear my hard work in person, not just on a phone recording."

He laughs and takes another swig of the beer. "Alright." He places the bottle on the foosball table. He gestures to the guys. "Let's take that one from the beginning, and I want Dave to start with that riff before we hit into the main intro."

The guys take their instruments and Chris counts them off from behind the drumkit.

Dave plays a really interesting blues lick and then the rest of the instruments come in. Rett is playing that old beat-up looking guitar, but it sounds amazing and it rings through the mix. Though I was hesitant – and maybe even a little defiant at first – to take on this project, hearing their music and the lyrics Rett and I wrote together makes it easy to forget that. I've heard a few more of the demo songs, and I know that this record is going to be huge for them.

They close out the song and I applaud. "Play 'Freebird'!" I say, laughing.

Rett flips me off. "We do *not* play 'Freebird,'" he says into the microphone, his voice echoing with reverb through the speakers. "What did you think?"

"I think it sounds like a first single," I say.

"Good, because we were thinking the same thing," he says, smiling.

Obviously it's up to the suits at Giant, but I think this song could be a huge hit.

I find a barstool in the kitchen to sit on as they play a few more songs. There's something about a man with a guitar that does something to me, no matter how much I try to convince myself otherwise. It's sexy and artistic, and I could definitely sit here and watch Rett and the band play all day.

"You guys are playing Mack's on Friday night?" I ask

as they finish up the last song of their session. They start putting their instruments away and winding up cables.

"Yeah," Clay says. "You're going to be there, right?"

"Of course," I say.

"Good. Because the last two shows you were at, we had complete sell-outs. So I think you might be a lucky charm," he says.

I laugh. "I don't know about that. I think your fans are just happy to see you playing live music again."

Once they have all of their gear put away, Rett motions toward the patio that's off the main living area. I follow him out, where there are a couple of folding chairs. A plastic bucket is filled to the rim of crushed beer cans.

"Thanks for coming to hang out today," he says. "I was starting to miss you."

My heart does a little flutter. "You run out of song ideas?" I ask sarcastically.

"Actually, no. After that first session, the floodgates opened. I've written so much in the last few weeks. I made photocopies, for you to take and tweak," he says, leaning against the railing of the tiny balcony. He takes a long draw from his beer and chucks the empty bottle into the bucket. It clings and clanks against the other empties.

"I've missed you too," I admit.

"I figured you've been busy taking care of Gabriela, so I didn't want to intrude," he says.

"Yeah," I say, turning away. "She's got a lot to figure out. That's actually why I decided to come out today. I needed to get out of the apartment. I needed to get away from it all."

"I feel that. Listen, I know this might be kind of weird, but I've been thinking about something. After the show Friday night, I'm driving back to South Carolina for a few days. I need to take care of some things at my dad's property. I'm planning on leaving Saturday morning." He looks at me. "I wanted to know if you'd like to go with me."

I don't know what to say. Go with him? "Wow," is all I can get out.

"It's okay if you can't. I know it's a spur of the moment thing. I was just thinking you'd like to see where I grew up. It could help with the songwriting stuff."

"No." I say.

"No?" He questions my response.

"That's not what I meant. Not no, as in I won't go. I meant to say, that sounds great. Wait, unless you're using me as free labor. There's laws around that sort of thing."

He laughs and shakes his head. "No. But I do need to do some fence repairs and rebuild a wall on the horse barn. A hurricane that came through last fall really messed up some stuff around the property, and I feel bad that I haven't been able to get down there to help get it repaired."

"I grew up on a ranch, Mr. Gordon," I say. "As long as you pay me well, I'm willing to work."

"How's room and board?"

I pause, faking serious consideration. "That'll work."

"Good." Rett reaches out and takes my hand. "It's a

deal."

His fingers interlace my own and I look up into his bright blue eyes. I forget where I am momentarily.

I could actually use some time away from Nashville, for a few days, to separate from Gabriela's situation. Doing something like building a fence, working with my hands, will be good to clear my mind and get some lucidity on what to do.

On top of that, I'll get to see what makes Rett tick, what makes him write songs the way he does. Where he draws his inspiration from.

The rest of the guys come out to the balcony and it gets crowded fast. Rett releases my hand. I feel his fingers slip from mine. My skin tingles in their absence.

"Did you ask her?" Clay says. Rett elbows him in the ribs.

"Yes he did," I say.

I know that they are getting ready for their show, but all I can think about is it being over. I'm ready for the weekend.

CHAPTER FIFTEEN

Rett

The show went without a hitch – another sellout, our third straight – and even better, we sold out of merch too. It feels nice to gain traction as we get ready to release this next record. I was worried that our last album had been buried by the pandemic, and we'd have to essentially start from scratch. Instead, it seems like the extended break and inability to play concerts just made our fans even more excited for us.

I wanted to leave early this morning, but once I picked up Nicole, made a coffee stop, and finally got on the interstate, it's after 8am.

The highway stretches out in front of us as we make a drive that I've not made in too long. Guiltily long.

Nicole grabbed a newspaper at the coffee shop, and she's in the passenger seat, her feet curled up beneath her as she's got it opened to the Entertainment section. She's wearing a large t-shirt and a pair of black yoga pants, but she's even more gorgeous than when she's all dressed up. There's just something about a woman who can do both, and do them well.

"MacKenzie Taylor is preparing a regional arena tour," she says, her face hidden between the thin pages of the newspaper. She drops it to her lap. "That would be cool if you guys could get something like that. You're already selling out theatres."

"Yeah, but I don't think Giant wants to pay for a tour like that for us. Not yet, at least. Maybe once the record comes out and we see the response."

"Ah," she says. "Gotcha."

I've got my phone connected to the Bluetooth on the truck's stereo, playing a playlist of some of my favorite old tunes. There's some Springsteen, some U2, a bunch of the music my dad listened to in the house when I was growing up. The music that made me want to play guitar, to start a band, to do what those guys were doing.

"You don't actually listen to a lot of country music, do you?" she asks.

"Not a lot, no," I say. "I listen to it to see what's popular, what the song structure is like, but when I want to put something on, it's usually this stuff. I'm always listening to new sounds, though."

"I do the same with poets, but sometimes I worry that I'll start emulating their style to the point that I lose my own."

"I read your book," I say. I picked it up at Parnassus Books downtown right after we met, and I read a few of her poems before bed every night. At first, I did it to get a feel for who I was working with. Then I read it, to get a feel for her.

"You did?" Her eyes go wide.

"Don't look at me like that. You know you're talented," I say. And she is. She's got a way with words, with making you feel emotions. Where I was once hesitant to work with her, I know now that she's our secret weapon.

"I still have a lot of doubts," she says. "But I appreciate the confidence boost."

"I know what you mean. I've probably felt at my lowest this year, fighting with writer's block. There were days, whole days, where I would just stare at a blank page. I could come up with chords, melodies, but nothing else. It was scary."

She nods. "And that kind of fear tends to capitalize on itself, stacking and stacking. You start wondering if you've written your last song, or if you only had one record in you."

It feels really good to be understood like that. As I drive, we talk nearly the whole time. At one point, she takes my phone and starts going through the Spotify playlists. The Beatles' "Day Tripper" starts playing.

"There we go," she says. "This reminds me of my childhood. My parents always had The Beatles on the stereo when I was a kid."

"I have to be honest, I never got into The Beatles. My

dad preferred the Stones, and I didn't really start listening to The Beatles until I met Dave in college."

"That's so funny," Nicole says. "My dad hated the Stones."

"I bet our dads will get along just great," I say sarcastically.

"Maybe."

"Maybe it'll be like us. Not like each other at first but then become best of friends."

"The kind of best friends that make out in the hallway of their apartment?" she asks.

"Jesus, I hope they don't," I say, nearly spitting out the water I'd just taken a drink from.

Nicole just laughs.

"What about your mom?" she asks, a subject I knew would come up eventually. A subject I'd been putting off for as long as I could.

"She died when I was young. Ovarian cancer." I just rip the band aid off instead of beating around the bush. There's no way to tip-toe around cancer.

"Oh my goodness." Nicole's eyes go wide with sorrow. "I'm sorry, I didn't know."

"It's okay. I don't really talk about her much. To be honest, I remember very little. Much less than I'd like. Like, I see pictures of her, when she was young, when my parents were newlyweds. But I don't really remember anything about those pictures."

"And your dad, he never remarried?"

"Nope. Spent the rest of his life raising a hellion son.

Now he spends his days on the property, feeding pigs and chickens," I say. "But even he's getting old now and the work is getting harder for him to keep up with." I give her a sideways glance and take her hand. She interlaces her fingers through mine. It feels like a perfect fit. "He's going to love you."

"Oh yeah?"

"How could he not?" I smile and she pulls my hand, the rest of my body following. Keeping one eye on the highway in front of us, I let her pull me in and she kisses me on the cheek. The Beatles continue to play and I'm happy.

* * *

All morning, we drove into the sun and as we pull up to the property, it's high above us. Just south of Chapin, the house sits on a nondescript two-lane road barely wide enough for a pickup truck. The house, white siding still chipping from the hurricane, stands out among a field of green. Trees line the property. As we turn into the gravel driveway that leads to the one-story cottage, one of my dad's dogs sprints out to the road and escorts the pickup, barking and jumping in excitement.

I park the truck and hop out, dropping to a knee to give the Golden Retriever a hefty rub behind his ears. He groans in response and licks at my arm.

"Good to see you too, Rooster," I say, standing.

My dad appears at the front door. He's wearing a pair

of denim overalls and a Rodney Scott's BBQ ballcap. His beard, close-cropped and littered with salt-and-pepper, gets saltier every time I see him.

"Boy, you made good time," he says, coming from the front door out to the drive. He still limps from a broken ankle he suffered nearly a decade ago, but rushes over and wraps me in a bear hug anyway.

"Good to see you, Dad," I say. "How are you feeling?"

"I'm doing alright," he says, patting me on the back. "How's the big city?"

"It's still there," I say.

Nicole steps out of the truck and my dad turns and does a double-take.

"I brought an extra pair of hands," I say. "This is Nicole."

"Well, hello." My dad's attention is immediately on her, and I could so much as vanish now, and he'd never know. I laugh as he takes her hand in a gentle handshake.

"Hi Nicole. I'm Buster."

"Nice to meet you, Buster," she says.

My dad turns back to me, her hand still in his. "Son, you didn't tell me we were going to have company."

"I didn't think you'd mind." I walk over to the passenger side of the truck and put my hand on his shoulder. "Nicole is helping me write the new record."

His eyebrows raise inquisitively. "Is that right?"

"Yes sir," she says, finally having her hand released from his grip.

"So you're a songwriter?" he asks.

"A poet, actually. But I was contracted by Giant Records to help polish the lyrics for Rett's new album."

"Figured a weekend trip to the ranch would give her some insight into who I am," I say.

"Well, if you want to know who he is, I've got plenty of stories," he says, with mischievous eyes.

"Now, now," I say, leading him to the house. "None of that. We're here to work."

"Well, y'all come on in. Let's make you something to eat." He starts for the house, opening the front door.

Once inside, it still smells like home. The front door opens into a living room that's decorated with modest furniture. A wood-burning stove occupies one corner, and there are pictures of my mother on the wall. The tops of the frames are dusty.

Further into the house, we get to the kitchen. A small round table where we had nearly all of our meals occupies a wide-windowed breakfast nook. The formal dining room was for decoration only. The only time it ever got used was when extended family came through for holidays.

My dad is standing in the open refrigerator, pulling out a pound of ground beef. "You're not one of those newfangled vegans, are you?" he asks. He's never been subtle.

"Dad," I say.

Nicole takes it in stride. "No sir," she says. "Born and raised on a ranch in Montana. Grew up on steak and eggs."

"A woman who can eat," he nods his head approvingly. "Hard to find these days."

Within a few minutes, he's got the griddle heated, a handful of hamburger patties patted out and sizzling on the hot surface. The plan is a quick lunch before getting out into the pasture and repairing the fence line.

Dad lays a spread out on the table – lettuce, tomatoes, onions, buns and cheese – and we build our burgers.

"So," he turns to Nicole. "Montana huh? What brought you to Nashville?"

"Change of pace," she says, and I notice that she's averting the question with a vague answer. "I'm excited to work with your son."

"We've actually got quite a bit of the new album written," I say, taking attention away from her and the obviously touchy subject that she's subverting. "In fact, I've got some of the demos in the truck if you want to hear them."

The old man grunts approvingly, his mouth full of burger. He chews and swallows. "Absolutely. You know, Everett gets his musical talent from my side of the family. The good looks, though, those came from his mother."

Nicole glances at me, her eyes sparkling from the light reflecting through the large bay window behind us, and I just want to lose myself in them.

"You two definitely cooked up a handsome one," she says. My dad's eyebrows raise and he looks at me. Now both of them are staring at me.

"What?" I ask. "It's obvious I didn't get these charming good looks from him!"

They both laugh.

After about thirty minutes, we clear the table. As Dad cleans up the mess in the kitchen, I pat him on the back. "I'm going to go ahead and get started on the fence."

"Sounds good. We'll be out in a few minutes as well."

"We?" I ask.

"Yeah. You go work. I've got stories to tell Miss Nicole here."

I groan and he laughs.

I leave them in the kitchen and make my way out to the shed, which is about forty yards from the house. It's a small barn — really more like a shed — that houses all the tools and equipment necessary for keeping up with the property. There's a riding lawn mower and chainsaws. I find the posthole diggers, a shovel, and a pair of canvas gloves. There's an old International Harvester hat hanging from a nail. I dust it off on my jeans and pop it on my head. It'll keep the sun out of my eyes and provide some shade as I work. Hitching the tools over my shoulder, I start for the far side of the property.

CHAPTER SIXTEEN

Nico

Montana is dry. The summers are warm, but tolerable. Easy to work outside. South Carolina, however, is an entirely different animal. It's so humid, I have sweat stains where I never have before, and I feel my hair frizzing out by the strand. I have it pulled back in a ponytail, but I feel it's as wide as my head now.

As gross as I feel, Everett looks incredibly handsome. The hat on his head is pulled backward, shading his neck. The sleeves of the plaid button-up he's wearing are rolled up, his tattooed forearms glistening in the dying sunlight.

"Alright," he calls out to me as he finishes hammering a metal fence post into the ground. "That's the last one."

We've spent the last few hours pulling out the posts that fell over from a hurricane and replacing them with new metal posts, staking them into the ground and reinforcing them so they'd be able to withstand a storm, if it were to happen again. As Rett pounds the posts, his Dad and I follow behind, tightening the replacement chain link panels.

Buster and I talk nearly the entire time, with Rett occasionally glancing at us disapprovingly.

"You make a good farm hard," he says behind me as he ties down the chain link. "We may keep you around."

"Oh yeah? Is this how your son gets help around here? Brings women as free labor?"

"Ha!" he guffaws. "He ain't never brought a girl home."

"Ever?" I ask, surprised.

"Nah. Not his style. Everett's always been more interested in making a name for himself. Don't want to get distracted, you know? He's always known what he wants, that boy."

I nod, and steal a glance at Everett, who's now leaning on the post hole digger.

"You two done gossiping about me?" he asks. He takes the hat off his head and wipes his brow on his sleeve.

Buster grabs the chain link tool, stretches the fence material over the final post, and I wrap a metal ring to keep it in place.

"All done," Buster says, pulling his hands out of his own leather work gloves. "I can't thank you two enough."

"Well," Everett says. "Done with this part. We still

have to fix the horse barn." He nods to a building near the other edge of the property. It looks like a lean-to, but one of the supporting walls is sagging, causing the whole structure to bow out.

"That's for tomorrow," Buster says. "It's getting dark. Time to start dinner."

"What're you cooking?" Everett asks.

"Well, I was thinking about firing up the grill, throwing some steaks on it."

"I haven't had a good steak in a long time. Hard to have a good cookout in the city."

Buster looks at me, as if he wants my approval. "That sounds perfect."

"Great," he says. "Let's go inside and clean up."

* * *

After dinner, we find ourselves out on the back patio, a deck made from 2x6 planks that Buster says he built himself, though Rett corrects him and says that *he* built it while his father "supervised." I love their relationship, and I can tell that not only is there a mutual respect and love, but there are decades of friendship between them. Buster throws another log into the brick-lined fire pit and the flames crackle in response. Up above, the stars are shining in a way that I've not seen since I left Montana, the Milky Way stretching across the sky. It feels like home.

The cool breeze from the ocean is salty but welcome

after spending all afternoon in the sun. Rett's cheeks are as red as mine feel, and despite being exhausted, the conversation is invigorating.

"Dad, you've got to come to Nashville soon. Especially now that everything is back open," Rett says. He's got a longneck bottle in one hand, a beer called Landshark.

"You know how I feel about the city," Buster says. He then turns to me. "This kid. Loves the city, but it's never been for me. Too many people, too much traffic."

"It's because he's a shitty driver and can get away with it when there's no one else on the road," Rett says, and I can't help but burst into laughter.

Buster looks like he's been insulted in the worst way. "Now you look here," he says. "I taught you how to drive."

"No," Rett says, "*I* taught me how to drive. You just gave me directions to the liquor store."

Buster shrugs and mutters something about, "Yeah, that's probably true."

"But seriously," I say. "Come to Nashville. You've got to listen to Rett's band before they blow up huge. This is probably the last time you'll get to see them play in the concert halls. This time next year, he'll be in arenas."

"Too loud," Buster says.

"This old man acts like he's ninety damn years old," Rett shakes his head. "Dad. You're sixty. Live while you're still alive."

"Yeah, maybe I'll come up there one of these week-ends," Buster says with a dismissiveness that is thinly veiled. He then stands up and stretches. "Guys, this old man is going to call it a night. We worked too hard today and we've got more to do tomorrow."

"Yeah," Rett says, finishing off his beer and tossing the bottle into a metal pail beneath his chair. "We should probably turn in as well."

I nod and agree, and as Buster douses the flame in the firepit, we head back inside the house.

After a shower, with Rett showing me how to work the knob – "It's finicky," he says – I'm in the spare bed-room, preparing to go to sleep. The lamp on the bedside table illuminates the room in a soft glow and it smells like cedar. There's a light knock on the door and I open it. Rett's standing in the doorway, in a pair of grey joggers and a white t-shirt. His tattoo is on full display. His hair is still wet from taking a shower after me.

He looks so damn sexy, and even though I try not to make it seem like I'm gawking, I don't think I am doing a very good job of hiding it. My heart is racing.

"Just wanted to tell you goodnight," he says quietly, almost a whisper. I realize I'm nearly leaning into him, and I can smell some kind of aftershave, almost like rum. It smells sweet and I want to inhale all of it.

"Goodnight," I say.

"Thanks for today."

"What do you mean?"

"I'm just saying. I know you probably weren't planning on spending your weekend working on a farm. But I appreciate it. And I love getting to spend so much time with you."

That electricity that fills my body shudders through my extremities with his words. "I grew up doing this kind of work," I say. "But I enjoyed doing it with you."

"I'll see you in the morning," he says, his forearm resting on the doorway.

"Sounds good."

I lean in and kiss him. He kisses me back, and I feel myself wanting to just melt into him, to wrap my arms and my legs and my whole being around him.

Rett places a hand on the small of my back and pulls me into him as his lips and tongue work their magic. My knees wobble as his kiss deepens. Our mouths move together, a slow and soft dance.

He releases me, and stares into my eyes. "Goodnight," he says one more time, capping it off with a tender kiss on the tip of my nose and then another on my forehead.

"Goodnight, Rett Gordon."

He leaves me in the doorway, holding onto the frame for support. When I feel like my legs will work again, I walk back into the room and shut the door quietly, my body full of heat and wonder, and a little magic of my own.

CHAPTER SEVENTEEN

Rett

The next day, we hop back into the truck and head back to Nashville. It'll be after dark when we arrive. I love driving into a city at night, all the lights and life that come into view. An inviting welcome.

It's always good to see my dad, though I worry about him being so isolated. Since I don't make it back often, he spends a lot of his time alone, save for the dogs. They are good companions but there's something to be said for human interaction, someone to share dinner with.

"I can't wait to sleep in my own bed," Nicole says, leaning back in the passenger seat of the pickup.

I've got a U2 album on, one of the ones from the nineties. The frantic danciness of the music, with its programmed drum tracks and loops, helps keep me alert. "I know what you mean," I say. "Sometimes there's nothing better than getting home and falling into your own sheets, even after just one night."

"Your dad is really sweet, and funny."

"He's mellowed out as he's gotten older. He was a hardass when I was a kid."

"My dad still is. Doesn't understand where he went wrong. Why his daughter wanted to move so far from home," she laments, though I can tell there's a lot of sarcasm there. Her father, in my opinion, didn't go wrong anywhere. This woman is the most intelligent, beautiful person I've ever met. And, if this weekend was any indication, she knows her way well around a ranch.

"Do you ever think about moving back?"

"I did at one point," she says. "When I was lost and didn't know where to go or what to do. It felt like going back home, would admit defeat. It would mean the people who hurt me had won. And maybe it's just me being hardheaded, but I couldn't face that. Gabriela talked me into moving to Nashville instead. She was able to get me in contact with Laura Van Hope. I was originally intending to be a songwriter procurement specialist. Find people to write songs for new artists, but then she suggested I put my skills to work. Then I got coupled up with you."

The last sentence ends with a smile, and I take her hand in mine.

"I'm glad that part worked out," I say. My mind sticks on the phrase coupled up. Are we a couple? I mean, we've kissed, more than once. But not much more than that, though I have thought about it more than I probably should. My imagination gets the better part of me when it comes to Nicole.

"Which part?" she asks.

"The last part, the end."

"Me too."

"I'm glad you ended up in Nashville, seriously."

"I never thought it was a place that I'd be, but it's growing on me. It's a fun town. I always thought it was just bachelorette parties and country music," she says. "Now that I think about it…that really is all there is!"

She laughs at her own joke and I do as well. It's no secret that Nashville is the bachelorette party capital of the world. There's not a night that goes by that you don't see a dozen sloshed bridal parties either weaving their way down Broadway, hopping from bar to bar, or worse, on one of those pedaling beer cars.

"There's also the Preds, and the Titans," I say. "And the Sounds."

"I know," she reassures me. "I'm just being silly."

Our friendly banter carries us the entire drive back to Nashville. Our hands graze steadily until they're intertwined.

"I'm more tired than I realized. All that manual labor. I'm not used to doing any more." Nicole rests her head on my shoulder as I drive.

I kiss the crown of her head and she nuzzles her soft and warm cheek into me harder. I feel so comfortable with her, in a way that I've not felt in a long time. It's not just butterflies in my stomach whenever I see her, there's an unexplainable peace that I feel whenever we're to-gether. Maybe it's because I don't think I have to impress her. She isn't trying to get with me because of who I am, and it's refreshing.

"Hey," I say. "Remember the first day we met?"

"Yeah, you weren't too pleased to see me in that boardroom."

"No," I say. "The day before."

She sits up and laughs again. "Oh my gosh. I wouldn't consider that meeting," she says. "But yes, at that coffee shop over off Broadway. Of course I remember. I was so disgusted. Not by you," she clarifies. "Well, partly by you. I just thought you were this smug country star, wading in a pool of women who were just throwing themselves at you."

"It's not my fault that they do," I say, with a slight grin.

Nicole punches me in the arm. "I'm glad I learned that that's not what you're about though. And I'm sorry for assuming so."

"It's a totally acceptable assumption to make," I say. "By the way, how did you know I'd be there?"

"I remembered reading an interview you did with *Nashville Living* about how you'd visit this place called Pal-ace Coffee on the mornings after a show, how it was, like, your 'recharge place' or something. I rolled the dice, hop-ing you'd be there."

"Likely story. You checked me out, but go ahead, call it research," I tease.

"I mean, maybe a little bit," she smirks. "What made you think of that day?"

"I was just sitting here, thinking about these last six weeks. At the beginning of it, I felt like I couldn't write, that I was stuck. And then you came along. Kicked me in the ass, so to speak. But, I just feel fortunate that you came along, whatever it was that brought you here."

"That's really sweet," she says, and she kisses me on the cheek. Her lips feel like heaven on my skin and I'm exerting all of my self-control not stopping this truck right now so I can kiss her senseless.

"Can I ask you something else? You don't have to answer if you don't want to, but your dad said something —"

I cut her off with a laugh. "He told you that you're the only girl I've ever brought around, didn't he?" I glance at her in the low light of the dark truck cab.

"Well, actually, yes."

"That's my dad."

"So…" she trails off. "Have you never had a girl-friend?"

I snort. "I've had plenty of girlfriends."

"Wow, that's cocky," Nicole says, sarcastically rolling her eyes.

I continue, "But, no. I've never brought anyone around to meet him. I was never sure about the future. I guess none of them were serious enough that I would want to sacrifice the band for a relationship. And I didn't want to bring anyone around if I knew the relationship was temporary in the first place."

Nicole doesn't respond. She just leans her head back on my shoulder.

We pull into Nashville, the city's downtown glowing off in the distance, growing closer with every mile. After making our way through traffic, I park in front of her apartment building.

"Do you want to come up for a little bit?" she asks.

"I mean, if you want me to," I say.

"My roommate texted when we were driving. She's staying with some of her model friends – long story. But, I could use a drink after all that hard work you put me through this weekend." She winks.

"I could definitely go for a drink," I say. Knowing that we've got the apartment to ourselves already makes the blood rush through my body and makes my heart flutter. I calm myself with a long exhale.

Turning off the truck, I grab Nicole's overnight bag from the backseat and follow her upstairs, where she unlocks the door apprehensively.

"Making sure Monster isn't going to attack us when we walk in," she says.

Once the coast is clear and it's evident that Monster is in some unseen hiding place, we walk in, and she turns on the lights. The living area is washed in a warm glow from the recessed ceiling lights.

"Where should I put this?" I ask, nodding to the tote in my hand.

"Oh, you can just set it down over there," she nods to

the doorway that leads to the hall.

I then follow her to the kitchen where she retrieves a couple of stemless wine glasses from the cabinets. She grabs a bottle of wine from the fridge.

"I thought we had some booze from a leftover party, but this is apparently the hardest thing we have," she says, displaying the bottle, the pinkish liquid inside.

I have steered away from wine for most of my adult life, except for one night in college where Clay and I found some Boone's Farm and spent the next day hungover and vomiting strawberry wine.

I shudder, and swallow the memory. "Sounds good to me," I say. "Just don't tell the guys."

She pours the two glasses and we hang out in the kitchen. She leans on the counter, cupping her wine in both hands. "My lips are sealed." She takes a sip and closes her eyes. "I'm so exhausted," she says.

"You and me both. Thank you for all your help this weekend. I didn't take you to make you do hard labor. I genuinely just wanted to hang out with you."

"I got to meet your dad, see where you came from. I call that research." Nicole grins wide and takes another sip.

"Oh yeah? A field trip to a farm in South Carolina, huh? I'm nothing but a research project now?" I say sarcastically.

She laughs, and scoots over to me, resting her head on my shoulder.

"You're more than that and you know it."

Had you told me when we first met that I would feel this way about her now, I would have laughed in your face. There was no way that Nico St. John and I would get along, but here we are. With her cheek nestled against my chest, sipping wine in her kitchen after spending the entire weekend together. This feels like home.

She lifts her head up and mine drops instinctively. Our lips meet, soft at first and then heavy. Her hands snake around the back of my neck and I wrap mine around her waist, pulling her into me. She kisses me harder, as her sweet wine-drenched tongue explores my mouth. I'm suddenly self-conscious, having spent the better part of the day in the truck, and I've not showered since this morning, but I toss the thought away. I am not going to let anything get in the way of this moment.

Wrapping my hands around the back of her thighs just below her ass, I lift and she tightens her legs around my waist, her hands still clasped to the back of my neck. She's breathing hard, heavy, like she's come up for air after being underwater for a very long time. Except she isn't breathing in air, she's breathing in me.

I turn and set her on the counter, my lips moving from the soft skin of her neck down to her chest. I reach my hands to her breasts and feel the lace fabric of her bra beneath her shirt.

"Oh my god," she cries, arching her back, as I continue my exploration of her body with my hands and lips.

I pull at her shirt, and she raises her arms in agreement. I toss the garment to the floor and bury my face between her breasts. I pop the clasp of her bra with one hand in a snapping gesture.

Nicole shimmies out of the bra and I take a moment to gaze at her perfect body. My god, she's gorgeous. Her ivory skin almost glows in the soft light of the kitchen and I can't help but stare in awe.

"Your turn," she says coyly, pulling at my plaid button-up. This is one of those times I wished I was wearing one of those pearl-snap shirts that I usually find at the vintage clothing stores downtown. Instead, I find myself awkwardly fumbling with the buttons until I finally get it removed. The white t-shirt beneath comes off much easier, and once I'm shirtless, I pull her close to me, devouring her gentle mouth once again.

I can feel the heat radiate as her body presses against mine. She moves her hands down to my belt and fumbles at it.

"Get these off," she says.

I start at my pants, start to obey her, but then move my hands to hers instead. I unclasp the button on her jeans and pull the zipper down, revealing a hint of pink cotton fabric.

"I don't even have my good underwear on," she whispers, almost apologetically, but I show her I don't care when I loop my hands into her waistband and pull her jeans down.

"Is this okay?" I ask.

"All the yeses," she says. She kicks off her shoes and I'm able to remove her jeans, depositing them on the floor next to our shirts.

She's in nothing but her panties and I run my hands over her bare legs. On full display for me now, I can't help but be amazed at every curve of her gorgeous body. I don't ever want this image removed from my brain.

I kneel at her legs, and kiss my way up her thighs. Grabbing the back of my head, she clasps her fingers in my hair and pushes me into her, but I make her wait for it. I kiss her inner thighs and snake my tongue at the barrier between her cotton panties and her womanhood.

"Oh my god," she says again. "Please stop teasing me."

"Never," I smirk, my hot breath penetrating her panties.

With a finger looped through the side of her underwear, I pull them to the side and let my tongue and lips explore all of her wetness. She writhes and calls out again, this time though, it's my name on her lips. I can feel her legs tense as she wraps them around me, her calves brushing against the back of my head. I lick and suck and feel her body move, feel her surrender to the pressure of my tongue.

Her fingers grasping at my hair, she pushes her hips into my lips. I relentlessly devour her until her calls become a desperate scream of release.

When her shaking subsides and her scream dies down to a few soft whimpers, aftershocks, I lift myself from between her legs and kiss her breasts and neck, wrapping my hands at the nape of her neck.

"Do you have protection?" she asks, her words heaving.

"Actually, I do, but," I pause. "They're in my bag. In my truck."

Nicole laughs at that, and I do too.

"I think Gabriela may have some." She hops off the counter and pulls me to her bedroom down the hall.

"Stay right here," she instructs, as she pushes me onto her bed.

I've not been in here, and it's tidier than I'd anticipated, though there's a rack of shoes on one wall, full to the brim of high heels and flats.

The décor is minimal but classy, prints in rose gold frames on the wall. The bed is soft and cool, but I know that it will be warm with fiery desire soon.

She returns, a package of condoms in hand. Smiling, she hands one to me.

"Your turn," she says.

Pulling my jeans off, she takes the wrapper from me and opens it. Within a few seconds, she's got it on, and she pushes me back on the bed.

"If it's okay, I'd like to do this," she says.

I'm okay with it, definitely okay with it. I nod my head.

Climbing on top of me, her legs sprawled on each side of my waist, she presses into me.

Then, fireworks.

CHAPTER EIGHTEEN

Nico

I wake up, the sunlight filtering through my window shades. Images of the night before fill my mind. I feel the blankets wrapped around my exposed body, as all my senses come alive again. I turn over, expecting Rett to be there, but he's gone.

I'm initially confused, but before I can run a thousand mental laps in my head about where he's gone and why he's left, I hear a rustling sound coming from the kitchen. In a few seconds, he arrives with a coffee mug in each hand. I could kiss him, but I really want a sip first.

"Good morning," he says with the cheerfulness of a man who spent all night having explosive and fun sex. "There were a few different creamers in the fridge, so I went with French vanilla."

"Great choice," I say, taking one of the mugs from his

outstretched hand.

He slips back into bed next to me. "Last night was…" he trails off.

"Amazing? Unexpected, but totally expected?" I finish for him.

Rett flashes that million-dollar-smile and takes a sip from his mug. "All of the above."

And, he's not wrong. It was amazing. That thing he did with his tongue sent me to the moon, and I can still feel my body reeling from quivering.

More than the sex though, was the fact that I was able to let myself open up to it. Perhaps it's because I was able to spend so much time with him that my guard was let down.

"I have a question, though," I say. "Why did you pack condoms in your bag?"

He laughs. "Oh man. I mean, I wasn't expecting it to happen, I don't want you to think that. But, I don't know. I didn't want to get caught off-guard in case it did. Like, the one-in-a-billion chance thing. I'd rather be prepared than not."

"That's an acceptable answer," I say.

He smiles again. "Good." He sips from his mug. The earthy, sweet aroma fills the room and the sunlight filters through the shades, illuminating rays of dust particles in the air. "I want you to know that I like you. I think you're really great, and you've helped me so much with my writing."

My heart jumps haphazardly in my chest. "I feel like

there's a but coming," I say, covering my nerves behind the rim of my mug.

"But," he says, "I understand if you're hesitant to be with me. Even though you haven't really detailed what brought you to Nashville, I can tell that you avert the question a lot. And I want you to know that I'm okay with taking things slowly. I'm okay if you ever feel like you need to be alone."

I don't really know how to respond to that. Rett is the first guy that I've felt comfortable around. I didn't feel like I had to second-guess what was in my coffee. He brought me coffee because he wants to be nice to me, not because he wants something from me.

I take in a deep breath. "It's not that I'm hesitant to be with you. When I was in Texas, I went out one night with the department head at the university. I was the writer-in-residence. Even though he was technically my boss, he was young, not even forty, and attractive."

Rett listens silently as I tell my story.

"One night, he asked if I wanted to have dinner with him. I agreed. We talked about Voltaire and Milton and Shakespeare. After dinner, we went to this pub. He kept giving me Long Islands. I woke up the next morning in his bed with no recollection of the night before. But it was clear that he…"

He takes my hand, and I realize in that moment that it's slightly trembling, the coffee in my mug making tiny waves. "It's okay," he says. "You don't have to tell me."

"It's just, that's why I couldn't be around you alone at

first. It was nothing you did. You were perfect. You took such good care of me when everything happened with Gabriela. But I woke up that next morning and you were in my kitchen and we were alone and I just freaked out. It triggered that memory, which tripwired my anxiety, and I didn't want you to see me at my worst."

He reaches over and kisses me on the forehead. It's comforting and sweet and feels like the thing I need most at this moment.

"I think you're more than great, Nicole. I think you're incredible, and I'm so sorry that happened to you," he says. "I promise, I will never hurt you."

I take another sip from my coffee and lean back against the fabric of my headboard. Being able to tell him my truth feels liberating. Like I can finally breathe. Plus, I don't know when I last was able to do this – relax in bed with a cup of coffee and feel totally at ease. I start to respond when a rustling noise beneath the bed jerks my head up and I turn to Rett, who has gone ghost-white.

"Is that the cat?" he asks.

"Oh no," I grumble, almost in unison with his question.

Then, out of nowhere, Monster shoots out from under the bed, a giant orange torpedo of hatred. I catch a glimpse of something in front of him. Something…

Grey.

"Oh shit, it's a mouse!" I scream. I try to place my coffee mug on the nightstand, but I miss and it lands on the carpet, beige liquid spilling everywhere, splattering the nightstand and the floor.

The mouse darts back and forth and Monster swats at it with his giant paws. Not only that, but he's making these demon cat sounds that could've only originated in hell, or wherever else Monster came from.

Rett jumps up on the mattress, not to survey the situation and do something about it, but because he is terrified of Monster. I can't help but laugh now, as he's standing on the bed in his boxer shorts, screaming at a cat.

"No!" he yells. "Bad Monster! Bad!" He continues to admonish the cat though to no avail. Monster slams into my shoe rack, causing multiple shoes to fall from it. The mouse avoids the falling shoes and skitters along the baseboard, though Monster quickly catches back up to it. The cat swats at the mouse, and this time he catches it. The mouse squeaks once before Monster is able to get it in his mouth. He shakes it violently, and then the little creature goes silent. Monster saunters out of the room with his prize, out the door and to the hall.

Rett gets up from the bed and goes to close the bedroom door. Coming back, he collapses on the mattress next to me, breathing heavy. My heart is going a million miles an hour. I turn to him, and I know my face is as ashen as his.

Suddenly, he starts laughing. Low at first and then heavy. I can't help but join him. I lean over and nuzzle into his chest, giggling. He wraps his arms around me.

"I've got to clean up this coffee," I say.

"I know. But first…" he pulls me into him and kisses

me again. I turn my body to fit into him and it's all over.

We awake again later in the morning, tangled in each other's arms, the sheets haphazardly tossed between us. My eyes blink open as my ears register the sound. It's a cellphone buzzing.

Rett gets up, groggily, and fumbles around for the device. It's in the pocket of his jeans that were abandoned on the floor last night.

He answers it and I take the opportunity to admire his body. In the light, I can see the muscles that were shaped not from hours in a gym but from working on a farm. His tan stops at his biceps, which means he earned it from being out in the sun. It's so sexy because everything about Rett is real and down to earth.

"Are you serious?" he says, his eyes bright and wide with excitement. "That, yes, that's…wow. Yes, thank you for the opportunity."

I don't know what's going on, but it must be something big, because I can see the almost boyish giddiness in his eyes and his demeanor. He disconnects the call and smiles.

"What was that about?" I ask.

"That was James from the label. Someone at the front office from the Nashville Sounds called," he says. "They want me to sing the National Anthem Friday night."

"That's amazing!" It would be a big chance to promote the band to tens of thousands of people. Though they're a minor league team, the Nashville Sounds draw nearly twenty thousand people on the weekend nights.

"So," he says, climbing back onto the bed and in between my legs. "Wanna go to a baseball game with me?"

"Are you asking me out on a date, Mr. Gordon?"

"Yes," he says, smiling. He leans in to kiss me. "Yes I am."

CHAPTER NINETEEN

Rett

The stadium is full of Sounds fans, with tons of activity on the berm and concrete walkways. As the seats fill in with fans, I sit on the field and take it all in. My bandmates are with Nicole in the Giant Records suite above the first base line. I find myself looking up there from time to time, trying to catch a glimpse of them, of her.

I've always wanted to do this, but never in my wildest dreams thought I'd actually have the chance to. It's more than getting to hang out on the field, seeing the warmups before the game up close, and taking part in the pre-game ceremonies. Singing the National Anthem before a baseball game is one of the highest honors a person can be given, and I take it seriously. I've practiced and rehearsed all week. It's a challenging song to sing, and it's even harder when you've got fifteen thousand people in complete silence, all those eyes on the flag waving out above centerfield and, of course, all those ears on you.

For a late spring evening, it's still warm and humid. As much as I love every second of this, I am only slightly envious of my friends who are already enjoying themselves in the air-conditioned suite, popping open beers and munching on the all-you-can-eat spread of baseball foods.

When I was a little boy, my dad would take me to minor league games – the closest major league team was the Atlanta Braves, but we never made it to see them in person. Instead, I was relegated to watching them on TBS. We'd go to Myrtle Beach to watch the Pelicans, and spend the weekend at the beach. At night, we'd watch baseball together, eating hot dogs and popcorn, and chasing foul balls. The smells of this place reminds me of that little beachside ballpark and it takes me right back to being ten years old.

On the guitar-shaped scoreboard in the outfield, I watch the players introduction video as the teams take the field. Then, a little kid, an eight-year-old cancer survivor named Kaylee, is escorted by the team mascot to throw out the first pitch.

The stadium's announcer calls out my name, the words echo through the ballpark. I'm about to sing the national anthem. The entire space goes so still and silent, the air vibrates. Sweat beads on my brow and in my armpits. I'm convinced everyone else can hear my heartbeat, its *thump thump thump* audible through the microphone that I'm holding to my chest. I realize how naked I feel without a guitar in my hands, protecting me like it always has. Now, I'm vulnerable and wide open. I feel so light, the wind might carry me away

I hold the microphone to my mouth and the first words pour out. There's a slight delay as the signal makes its way through the speaker system, but I'm able to drown it out and keep going.

Ninety seconds later, I finish the anthem, bellowing, "And the home of the brave!" to a raucous applause. Fireworks shoot off in the outfield, red and blue plumes of light. I breathe a sigh of relief and hand the microphone to the stadium attendant. I'm escorted off the field and to the steps to the suite level.

I'm greeted with outstretched hands of people wanting to high-five and congratulate me on a job well done. I stop for a few selfies and autographs. After nearly fifteen minutes, I finally make it up to the suite where my friends are waiting. The game has started in earnest, and by the time I get up to the suite, it's the middle of the first inning.

"Good job, my man!" Clay shouts, as I step in. He pulls me into a big bear hug and I'm once again reminded of the sweat under my shirt. It makes the fabric stick to my body as he lets me down.

Nicole approaches as well. "You did an amazing job," she says.

Even with my other bandmates and label execs giving

me props, her words mean the most. I want to pull her in for a kiss right here, but I decide to keep our relationship subtle for now.

"Mr. Gordon," a voice from behind me says. "That was an incredible showing. Just…wow."

I turn and am faced with a petite blonde woman, her hair in ringlets. I immediately recognize her from the billboards and the music videos.

MacKenzie Taylor.

She's much shorter in person than I'd anticipated. If it weren't for the three-inch heels on her feet – black with red soles – she'd barely top out at five feet. Gone, though, is the soft country star look that she sported in the past. Her hair is done up and she's covered in glitter. She looks like a pop star.

"Thank you," I say, the words taking a lot of effort to get out. I feel out of my element now, with this actual country star right here, in our suite, watching a baseball game with us. It feels surreal.

"Did you get my gift?" she asks.

I cock my head, puzzled. "Gift?"

"Yeah," she says. "David at the label told me you were starting work on your second album. Which, by the way, the first one is amazing." She almost sings the last word, her voice going high-pitched. "And I know when I write, I like to use a good notebook, so I had one sent to you."

"That was you?" I say, incredulous. "What? How? Why? I mean, thank you. Speaking of writing, you should meet Nico. She's helping me write the album." I catch

Nicole's attention as she's standing on the balcony of the suite that looks down onto the field. I motion for her to come over.

"MacKenzie, this is Nico St. John," I say.

The women shake hands, and it's a fake cordiality that is so palpable it fills the room.

"Ah," MacKenzie says, "the poet, right?"

"Yes," Nicole replies.

"Well, just don't let Rett here lose his voice. Second albums are where the career is made, and we wouldn't want a sophomore slump." Though she says it with a smile, it's like the grin of a predator before it pounces on its prey.

"Why don't we," I suggest, motioning to the balcony, "go sit and watch the game?"

"That sounds great," Nicole says. Her eyes stay on MacKenzie.

"I may stick around for an inning or two, but I really do have to get going soon. I only wanted to come watch you sing the anthem. We are finishing rehearsals for this tour, as you probably know, and there's just so much left to do," MacKenzie says. She keeps her attention on me, as if pretending Nicole isn't even there.

"Well, sounds like you're a busy woman. We wouldn't want to keep you," Nicole says.

MacKenzie turns to her and flashes that feline grin, "Like I said, perhaps an inning or two."

The Sounds win in dramatic fashion, with a walk-off three-run homerun from their power-bat first baseman, and as I drive Nicole back to her apartment, I've got her hand in mine. The radio is turned up, and one of MacKenzie's songs comes on.

"Can you switch the station?" she huffs.

I turn the dial and find a station playing Journey. "She's definitely full of herself, yeah?" I ask.

"A little bit. I don't think I've ever met someone so self-obsessed. I mean, I'm pretty sure she took thirty selfies in the two innings she was there."

"Were you counting?"

Nicole glares at me. "No. But you know what I'm saying."

I take her hand and give it a squeeze. "I think that's what happens when you become a celebrity so young. I mean, she's been doing this music thing since she was fifteen years old."

MacKenzie Taylor was, what we call in the industry, a ten-year overnight success. Her first few albums sold decently enough, but it was when she started crossing over to more pop that she found a mainstream audience.

"Well, just promise me you won't ever be so vain. Ugh. And the way she called me *the poet*, like it was some ratchet thing." She turns to me now, one leg propped up in the seat. "I'll have her know that I was a finalist to present at Barack Obama's first inauguration when I was still an undergrad. I was Writer in Residence at SMU in Dallas. I have actual accolades, not just a bunch of teenyboppers who think I'm fake famous because I know how to use an Instagram filter."

She seems really perturbed, and it's kind of cute, actually. But it also reminds me of how hard she has worked in her career, and how much pride she takes in it. I understand that work and that pride. I feel the same thing with the band and our music, which is why I was so hesitant and militant toward Nicole when we first started working together.

I give her hand another reassuring squeeze. "I'm sure she didn't mean it like that."

"You're probably right. She's just so self-obsessed that she can't see the rest of the world around her."

"I don't think I've ever seen you this upset. Well," I pause, thinking about that first morning after we'd gotten back from the emergency room and she kicked me out of her apartment. "Except for that one time."

"What time?"

I remind her, gently, about leaving the morning after we returned from the hospital, confused.

She rolls her eyes. "I apologized for that already, Mr. Gordon," she says, putting emphasis on my name. "I knew I was already into you, but just had a bit of an anxiety attack."

I laugh and squeeze her hand. "It's all okay," I say. "That was a long time ago." I smile and pull her into me, kissing her on the forehead. "By the way, I was really into you too. I am really into you."

She closes her eyes and stays resting on my shoulder

as I drive. I feel her calm down as she nuzzles into me.

"Hey," I say, apprehensively. "Would you want to come back to my place? For the night?"

She sits up. "Are you sure?"

"Yes," I say. "Yes I am." This is a barrier I'm ready to break with her. I've never had a woman go back to my apartment. It helps me stay sane, hoping that I won't have to deal with crazy stalkers or ex-girlfriends who know where I live.

"Okay. Can we stop at my place first? So I can grab some stuff."

"Of course."

I take the exit from the highway that leads to her apartment, and when we pull up, I wait in the truck as she goes inside. As I sit there, I scroll through my phone, looking at pictures from the evening. My phone dings and a Facebook messenger notification pops up on the top of the screen. I see MacKenzie's name at the top of the screen.

It was so nice finally meeting you tonight!
Sorry I had to run so early.
I really wanted to hear more about your album.

I swipe down and type out a response.

Thanks for your support.
Good luck on tour.

I lock the phone and shove it in one of the empty cup-holders in the center console. Nicole exits the building and jogs back to the truck on the sidewalk, an overnight bag slung over her shoulder.

"Okay," she says, and she kisses me again. "Ready to go."

My phone buzzes again in the cupholder as I put the truck in drive and head to my apartment, but I leave it there, ignoring it. I don't want any more distractions tonight.

With the electricity already between Nicole and me, I'll be distracted enough as it is.

CHAPTER TWENTY

Nico

The smell of coffee fills my senses as I wake in Rett's bed, and I'm not surprised when I roll over to find that his side of the sheets are empty. Unlike the first time we spent the night together, it doesn't fill me with dread or make my anxieties skyrocket. Instead, it's peaceful.

My phone is on the nightstand, and I grab it to check the time. It's just after eight in the morning, but my device is almost dead. I get up, and scrounge around for my bra. It, like the rest of my clothes, are scattered on the floor. You can almost see the trail, like a sexy Hansel and Gretel, from where we started making out in the hallway to the bedroom, with clothes littered all along the way.

I actually smile. I haven't felt like this about someone in a long time, and I didn't think I'd ever allow myself to be so vulnerable with someone again. I find a large t-shirt in one of Rett's drawers and throw it on, and then tie my hair up in a bun on top of my head.

Following my nose, I make my way to his kitchen. He's got some kind of music playing from an Alexa device on the counter and he's humming along to it. With his back turned, I simply watch for a few seconds, completely enamored as he works a spoon in a bowl.

"Good morning," I say, as I make my way to the kitchen. He turns at my words and smiles.

"That," he gestures to the shirt, "looks damn good on you."

I look down at the graphic on the front. It's a Bonnaroo Festival shirt from a few years ago.

"It was just the first thing I pulled out of your drawer, but maybe if you're good I'll give you a fashion show later with the rest of your wardrobe," I say.

Rett laughs at that. Setting the bowl down on the counter, he pulls a mug from one of the cabinets above the sink and pours me a cup of coffee. He's already got a bottle of cinnamon vanilla creamer out and he slides it over as well.

His kitchen is a lot like mine, and probably a lot of the other modern apartments in downtown Nashville. Instead of marble, the countertops look like stained concrete, and the appliances are all stainless steel. Though the kitchen itself is small, it's open to the larger living area. The ceiling is high and has a really cool warehouse feel. As I take it all in, I see the wall decorations, which are guitars on wall mounts.

"What are you making?" I ask.

Taking the bowl back into his hands, he continues a mixing motion. "Liege waffles."

Oh my god. Yes. I love liege waffles and I immediately make a moaning sound that makes Rett laugh. Liege waffles are heavy, thick waffles full of pearl sugar and usually piled high with fruit and whipped cream. They're also probably thousands of calories, but I don't care.

"I take it you like liege waffles?" he says.

"Oh yes," I nod, taking a sip from my coffee.

It occurs to me how much I enjoy this, waking up to Rett cooking breakfast, hanging out the morning after we've lost ourselves in each other all night. He is as good in bed as he is in the kitchen, and I am lapping it all up.

"Good," he says as he sets the bowl back down on the counter. He covers it with a white kitchen towel and tosses the wooden spoon into the sink. Grabbing his own mug, he comes around the counter and kisses me on the cheek. "I'll be right back."

"Hey, while you're back there, do you have a spare phone charger? My phone is almost dead," I say. I hold the device up and show him the red battery status.

"Absolutely. Give me one second."

He goes to the bedroom and comes back a few seconds later, a coiled phone charger in one hand and his songbook in the other.

The songbook, I discovered, was given to him by MacKenzie. That thought shouldn't make me jealous, but it does. I can't help but wish that it had been me that gave him that notebook that he's written so many words in lately. I know he's proud of the book, and proud of the work that he's done in it, but it just fills me with this sour feeling knowing part of it includes any part of her.

He plugs the charger into a receptacle on the wall next to the counter and hands me the tip. Then, he opens up the notebook.

"I have a few more songs, but I'm having some issues with one of them. I just feel like I can't get the story right."

I turn the notebook so I can read it. His handwriting, scratchy and in several different pen colors – blue striking out black, red scribbles in the gutters – fills the pages, both front and back. There are the lyrics as well as little notes he's made to himself. Some words are repeated over and over, thematic elements that I can tell he's working with.

Though Rett is writing music, he writes like a poet, and it helps me fall into a comfortable rhythm when working with him. I turn the pages, reading his words, his lines.

"What does this mean?" I ask, pointing to some letters in the gutter between the pages. Some of them have what look like hashtags next to them.

"Oh, that means what key I hear the melody in. So, that means it's in C sharp."

"Ah," I say. "Can you sing me the melody?"

He hesitates.

"That way, I can hear the rhythm that you hear inside

your head," I say.

He hums the words quietly, averting his eyes from me and keeping them on the page.

"Don't be embarrassed," I say.

"I just don't like singing in front of other people," he says.

I laugh. "What do you mean? You sing in front of other people all the time. You literally sang in front of fifteen thousand people last night."

"Yeah, but that's a whole crowd. I know it probably sounds stupid, but I don't get nervous in front of a crowd, because it's a crowd. But, if I have to sing for a roomful of people, if it's something small, I get nervous. I can't do it."

"What if you just imagine them in their underwear?" I lift my shirt a bit and flash the side of my black lace underwear.

Rett laughs. "Oh, so then I have to sing while being completely turned on?"

"Well, just hum it then," I say, nudging against him.

He puts an arm around me and I lean against his chest. With the notebook open on the counter, he hums the melody and I follow along.

"I like this one," I say. The story of the song is about a hometown boy who falls in love with a girl who no one else pays attention to. It's radio fodder for sure, but the melody is catchy. It's got a hook. "Can I suggest one small change though?"

"Of course you can," he says. "That's literally what

you're being paid for."

"I know. I just still feel weird about it. If someone asked to change one of my poems, something I poured my soul into, I'd tell them to kiss my ass."

"Well, you're not just someone. I trust your judgment."

I nuzzle against him again and smile. "Okay, so this line at the end when he realizes he's in love with her, right before the chorus again, I think you should change the wording to the antonyms of the first verse. So, thematically, and lyrically, it comes full circle."

"Oh, yeah," Rett says, his eyes wide. "I like that."

"Do you have a pen?"

Rummaging through one of the drawers beneath the counter, he produces a pen.

I scratch out some lines and write in a new verse. I let him read it.

"That's good. That's really good."

"I think this one has got radio hit written all over it," I say.

"Good," he says. He takes another sip of his coffee as he re-reads the words. "We're recording it for the studio demo this week. And then turning the demos in for review."

"Oh wow," I say. "That's exciting!" I can't believe that they're already at the stage where they can start showing the studio the demos.

"Yeah," he says. "I'm still…" he trails off.

"What?"

"I had nearly a decade to write that first album, you know? I worked on those songs for years. This time, it just feels like it's happening so quickly, that I don't know if I'm putting my best work out there," he says.

"You doubt yourself a lot," I say. It's an observation, not an insult. "But you shouldn't. You are talented, both with the music and with the lyrics."

The open living room has a large window that looks out onto downtown Nashville, and he stares out at the burgeoning awakening of the day. He puffs out a sigh, his cheeks filling with air. It makes him look like an adorable chipmunk.

"There's so much riding on a second album. If it doesn't sell, we're done for."

"These songs," I say, tapping my finger on the notebook, "are really good. And the label will think so as well. Remember, I have a lot riding on this too. I'm not going to let you release a shit album with my name on it."

He smiles again, and pulls me in for another hug. I lean my chin up for a kiss when his phone rings. The kiss doesn't last as long as I'd like it to, but he pulls away to grab the device from the counter and answers it.

I motion that I'm going to walk down the hall so I can let him take his call in private. Back in the bedroom, I clean up our mess and fold my clothes from the night before, placing them with my overnight bag. After a few minutes, I go back to the kitchen.

Rett's leaning against the counter, his head in his hands.

"What's going on?" I ask. "Are you okay?" He looks like he's in pain.

"Yeah, it's just," he says. "That was the label."

My heart sinks. Why would someone from the label call on a Saturday morning?

"What's wrong?"

"They just said to clear our schedule and that we've got a meeting scheduled Monday morning."

"To talk about the album?"

"No," he says. "To talk with a tour promoter."

"That's great!" I say. Though, if the label wants a record finished before November, I don't know why they'd schedule a tour.

"MacKenzie Taylor's tour promoter," he says.

And, for reasons that I can't explain but totally understand, my heart sinks.

CHAPTER TWENTY-ONE

Rett

"So let me get this straight," I say. "You want us to go on tour for five weeks while trying to record an album."

"Yes."

The simple response from Laura Van Hope is both frightening and exciting.

She takes a sip of water from a glass on the conference table and continues. "You will be the supporting act for the first leg of the tour. What we're hoping, is that it generates regional buzz for the new album before the first single release."

"Yeah, I got that the first time you said it, it's just that I feel like we'd be cutting it close. You're asking us to take five weeks away from recording. Not only that, but two weeks of rehearsals? We just finished the demos."

I look to Clay on my right. Chris is on the other side

of him and Dave is to my left. They all have the same look of incredulity on their faces. Almost as if what Laura Van Hope is asking of us is both a dream come true and a logistical nightmare.

Across the table from us is Daniel Valencia, the manager of the company running MacKenzie's tour. He's a large man in an ill-fitting suit. His hair is slicked back and he looks like an extra on The Sopranos. His voice is gruff, like a used car salesman who's been rejected one too many times.

"With Ben Knotts backing out of the tour, we need someone who will add excitement to the bill. MacKenzie is enough of a draw, don't get us wrong, but we need you guys to bridge that gap between the country and the pop audiences. Plus, Miss Taylor requested you specifically. She wants The Last Train Home on this tour."

It's no secret in the industry that MacKenzie's latest record, though a huge success, was incredibly divisive. It was more produced, more pop-ish than anything else she'd previously done.

But it catapulted her into this kind of arena tour. Now it's intertwining us into it.

I feel like I'm looking the gift horse straight in the mouth, wondering if it's going to swallow me whole.

"The fact of the matter is," Laura Van Hope says, "is that this is mutually beneficial for everyone involved. The demos you submitted show us that the album is heading in the direction we want it to go, and it's obvious that

Nico St. John's influence has helped with the lyrical content. We want to get these songs in front of audiences now, which will generate excitement for the album. We have no doubts that by this time next year, it will be Rett Gordon and The Last Train Home headlining this style of arena tour."

I can't help but let that idea fill my head with images of huge crowds screaming for us. Seas of people buying tickets to the shows.

For the first time since the meeting started, Clay speaks up. "If we agree to this tour, we need to discuss compensation. You're asking us to give up five incredibly valuable weeks of recording time. Five weeks that could make or break this album."

I nod, seconding his sentiments, and his sensibilities bring me back down to earth. His ability to stay rational is something I admire and envy.

"Clay's right," I say. "I understand that this tour will generate buzz, but the fact of the matter is, this album isn't anywhere near complete. The songs could change drastically between now and the studio, and you're asking us to give up valuable workshop time."

"Not at all," Laura Van Hope says. "You'll be able to workshop the songs live, in front of an audience."

I can't argue with that. If anything, playing the new songs night after night will make them tighter and better.

"Still, Clay is right. We would want to be fairly compensated." I've heard too many horror stories about supporting acts playing for peanuts on this kind of tour.

I feel like we have an upper hand here, though. The tour promotion company and the label need a replacement for Ben Knotts, and they need it quickly. I realize that it's a perfect storm. Time to sink or swim.

"What do you think is fair?" Valencia asks.

"Fifteen percent," Clay says. Even I gasp.

"Okay," Valencia says, nearly choking on a sip of water. "Let's come up with something more reasonable."

"You said it yourself," Clay continues, all business mode now. "MacKenzie specifically requested us. You need a band who is tour-ready, with material to promote. We're the only thing you've got. We're giving up time to record, so you're asking Ms. Van Hope and all of Giant Records to take a risk by having us out on tour with MacKenzie. Fifteen percent is more than fair."

As he negotiates, I do some quick math in my head. If each arena holds ten thousand people, fifteen percent is close to sixty grand if each ticket averages forty dollars. The back of my neck gets sweaty just thinking about that.

"Fifteen percent is the kind of number reserved for headliners," Valencia retorts indignantly.

Clay simply shrugs. "We've got a lot of work to do," he says.

Laura Van Hope speaks up. "I do believe that we can come up with a mutually beneficial number for everyone involved here. What are you thinking, Daniel?"

"Common practice is two percent," he says, his eyes narrowing our direction.

"For two percent, we'd be more than happy to finish

our record," Clay volleys. "But thank you for wasting our Monday afternoon. I could still be asleep right now."

"Settle down, Mr. Shepherd," Laura says. She turns back to Valencia. "Two percent may be typical, but this is an atypical situation. Why don't we settle for eight percent, with the promise that Valencia Promotions will be the exclusive promoter of the band's first headlining tour after the album release."

Valencia stands up, pausing. "I think that's reasonable."

However, I have gone temporarily deaf. Our first headlining tour? After the record? We're going to headline a concert tour? Holy shit. My hands immediately go hot and slippery. It's finally happening. We're going to be a headliner, on our very own tour.

Clay nudges me and I stand up with him. The four of us all shake hands with Valencia. Laura Van Hope congratulates us all and we're eventually led out of the conference room, with the assurance that contracts will be sent out within the next twenty-four hours.

I walk out of the office and toward the elevator with my band. We get in and let it take us to the ground level, none of us saying much. The silence between us suddenly erupts into laughing and high-fiving. It's settled. We're going on tour with MacKenzie Taylor.

And we're going to make a fortune doing it.

* * *

The bucket of beers is now full of empty bottles and the waitress comes to replace it with a fresh one. If our first concert after the pandemic felt like we were back, this feels like we've made it. Sure, we're just an opening act, but an opening act on a tour in front of tens of thousands of people every single night.

It's also admittedly really scary. By agreeing to this tour, even if it's just a five-week leg, we're taking away valuable recording time from the album. I feel like we've hit a stride in writing the record, and Nicole and I have been working together really well. Any shift in the routine could change that stride.

Despite that, we're all smiles at the table on the patio at Mack's. Mack's is one of the more upscale restaurants downtown, with a rooftop patio that looks down on the city streets below. There's a ton of work to do, and limited time to do it, but for now, we're celebrating.

Chris pops open one of the beers from the new bucket and takes a large swig. "I just can't believe we're going on tour with MacKenzie Taylor. You think she already knew when she was at the baseball game Friday night?"

"Yeah, Rett," Dave says, turning to me. "She seemed like she was a big fan. I thought she was going to go groupie status on you."

"No, no," I say, shaking my head. "Nothing like that. And, I don't know. If anything, I think she knew that the tour needed a new opening act, and she wanted to get a feel for how we all are together."

Even Clay looks at me disbelievingly, like I'm trying to sell a truck with no engine in it. The explanation has no gas.

I switch the subject. "The tour will be a great opportunity to work on these songs in a real setting, hearing them in an arena will show us how they really sound."

With Nicole's help Saturday morning, we finished two more songs, which gave us the entire album. After eight weeks, it was finally written. Barring any major changes, the record is ready to demo to the label – a process that will now have to wait.

"Look man, you don't have to sugar-coat and bullshit us," Clay says. The other guys nod. "She's into you and pulled some strings to get us on the tour with her."

"Well, whatever it is, it's a good opportunity for us." I take a sip from the beer bottle in my hand. I've been nervously chipping away at its label with my thumbnail and little strips of wet paper have flaked off.

"A good opportunity or a chance for everything to blow up in our faces," Dave says.

"What do you mean?" I ask.

"I mean, we definitely want to go on tour, but the timing is pretty bad. The label is pushing for this record, pushing for us to go on tour to generate buzz, and if there's anything MacKenzie Taylor likes, it's a spotlight. That spotlight will be on us now, too. And it's a bright one."

"Yeah," is all I can muster.

My phone dings, and I hope it's Nicole. I texted her a bit ago, telling her the details of the meeting and invited her to join us here at Mack's. Instead, it's an email with a contract for the tour. I'll have Clay read it over and have his dad, an attorney who still lives in Murfreesboro, give it the once-over before we sign anything. I put the phone back in my pocket and return to the conversation.

"I like to see this opportunity for what it is – an opportunity," I say. "We didn't start this band to play concert halls in Nashville for the rest of our careers. We knew we wanted to be big, to sell records, to play arenas. Now's our chance. It may not be the way we envisioned or would have wanted, but we have to take the punches as they come. This is going to catapult us to that next level. We've done a fantastic job so far, but the label sees bigger things for us, and frankly, so do I."

"I agree with you," Clay says. "Those spotlights that Dave was talking about, they can be blinding. We just want to make sure that we're doing this for the right reasons."

Clay's always been practical. Part of his upbringing and part of his natural disposition. If I'm the sail of the band, he's the anchor, making sure we stay in place when we need to. But, right now is a time for going with the wind.

"It's just five weeks," I say. "Five weeks and we're all richer and have thousands of new fans. Fans who will come back when we are the headliners."

The rest of the guys nod in understanding.
I raise my beer. "Til the last train home."
They clink their bottles against mine.

CHAPTER TWENTY-TWO

Nico

My phone dings with a text from Rett. I put the phone back on my desk. My laptop is open to an application for the University of Montana, and my fingers feel heavy as they type out the answers on the form.

For all intents and purposes, my job here in Nashville is done, and it wouldn't make sense for me to stick around. I remind myself that Nashville was never meant to be a permanent move, but something that would help me regroup.

Despite all the rationalizing I do in my brain though, I can't help but feel something like guilt. As much as I try to push it to the back of my brain, it stays there, gnawing away at my resolve as I slowly push through filling out this online application.

I wasn't looking to leave, but when the job opening

came available, I couldn't ignore the timing of it all. It felt like a sign, a sign telling me it was time to move on.

I've always desired to return to my alma mater, back to the one place that has always felt like home. It was my home, until I thought that anywhere else other than Montana was home.

The sad thing is, I was beginning to think Nashville could be my new home. When we were kids, Gabriela and I always talked of moving to a big city together when we "grew up." Though we thought it would be New York or Los Angeles, Nashville has been amazing. And working with Rett, getting close to him, has made me believe things could work here. That I could be happy. But, when I pull myself away from the emotional part, I know that my relationship with him and with this city was meant to be temporary.

My phone dings again, and again it's Everett, again.

Hey, come hang out with us.

I sigh and type out a reply.

I wish I could, but I'm really busy.
How did the meeting go?

The three bubbles pop up, signifying his response.

It went great. Really exciting.
Going on tour!

He's going on tour with MacKenzie Taylor. That is the new reality of our situation. I can't even think about all of the selfies, of them together, of Rett traveling, having the time of his life. It will be plastered all over social media, a constant reminder of what I maybe could've had with him.

What am I even talking about? I push away from my laptop and look around my empty room. There's no way Rett would ever choose me over her. Once they're on the road together, it'll be like I never existed. Out of sight, out of mind.

She's a star, a musician like him. They have that connection. We're just friends, I guess. Not even that.

We're coworkers.

Coworkers, who occasionally have mind-blowing sex.

And make breakfast in the morning afterward.

Followed by more mind-blowing sex.

I don't even know what I should say to him. I'm so confused. Too many thoughts are racing through my brain, around and around in circles, spiraling and collapsing on each other. It's not like we're breaking up. That would insinuate we were a couple in the first place. And we never talked about that. He never said those exact words to me. So, why did it feel like we were?

"Ugh," I blow a frustrated breath out.

"What's wrong?"

Gabriela's voice behind me makes me nearly jump out of my chair. I clutch my chest and instinctively shut my laptop.

"What, are you looking at porn?" she asks. There's a smile across her face, something I haven't seen in a long time.

"No," I retort, swiveling around, "I'm not looking at *porn.*"

"Nine times out of ten, if someone shuts their laptop like that, it's because it's porn." She comes into the room and sits on my bed. She's still smiling, almost beaming.

"Why do you look so happy?" I ask.

"You're not going to believe this, but I found a foster home for Monster," she says.

I feel my jaw go slack. "You're right," I say. "I don't believe it. Who?"

"This sweet girl from the Van Hope Group," she says. "You may even know her. She works for the label, the receptionist."

I do know who she's talking about, the redhead at the front desk.

"Why would she want Monster?" I ask. That cat is a demon, lurking and waiting to strike from whatever hiding place he can find.

"She had a cat a lot like him apparently. Her sister works with us. Anyway, long story short, she knew that we were just holding onto him, waiting to find him a forever home, and she wants him."

This is great news, and just one more thing that makes leaving Nashville and going back to Montana that much easier.

"Awesome," I say. The smile on my face is forced, and Gabriela calls me out on it.

"What's going on?" she asks.

Before I can even answer, she cuts me off.

"And don't give me that nothing bullshit. You look like you've gone through a breakup."

That's the thing. I feel like I have. Rett's leaving, for who knows how long. Now that the record is written, there's no reason for us to spend so much time together. This whole situation is a train wreck speeding a million miles an hour in my head.

"It's not nothing, it's definitely something, but I don't even know how to explain why I'm so upset. Rett and his band are going on tour with MacKenzie Taylor and—"

She cuts me off. "Oh wow! That's exciting!"

"For him, yeah. I don't know. I just feel like he and I have something special, and it's being taken away. I won't get to see him for who knows how long. And I don't like MacKenzie Taylor. You should've seen her at the Sounds game. She was all over him, like a groupie. It was gross."

Gabriela raises her eyebrows. "Nicole," she says. "Are you…jealous?"

"No," I retort. "Yes. It's just, we've spent so much time together. He was there for me, and for us, when you were in the hospital. And I felt like we have something. But maybe, it was all just to get this record written. Now that that's done, he doesn't need me anymore."

"Maybe you're overthinking this a little? Like everything else in your life?" she suggests.

My phone dings again, another text from Rett.

Come party!

It's four o'clock in the afternoon on a Monday and he and his bandmates are partying. I could never keep up with that kind of lifestyle. As much fun as Rett is to be around, I just don't want that life.

"I'm not overthinking it. I'm being rational. Realistic. He's a musician, and he has to go on tour to make a living. I do not. I need something more grounded."

"Do you believe that, or are you just making excuses?" Gabriela raises an eyebrow.

I huff in response. "What's that supposed to mean?" I ask indignantly.

"That maybe you're still running from being hurt in the past, and you're guarding yourself from that happening again – whether it does or not?"

"You're one to talk," I say, and immediately know that it's the wrong thing to say. Gabriela's face goes slack and she averts her eyes.

"That's not fair," she says.

I double down. "When are you going to confront Max about what he did to you? When are you going to take a stand against him and stop ignoring the fact that he took advantage of you and you got pregnant?"

Gabriela bursts into tears and storms out of the room. I feel like an asshole, but I'm not ready to admit that to her or to myself. Instead, I grab my purse and leave. I want to be alone, but I also know what I need to do.

CHAPTER TWENTY-THREE

Rett

Well I'm buzzed, on alcohol and the excitement of the tour. Chris has his phone out and he's looking up statistics of MacKenzie Taylor's last tour and trying to do math about what our cut would potentially be from the upcoming five-week jaunt, but he's having a hard time doing math with four beers in him. We are all laughing at the incredulousness of all of it. Just a few months ago, we were excited to be back out just playing the local circuit. Now, I'm looking at the potential venues that we'll be playing, venues that hold tens of thousands of people, instead of the three or four thousand we generally play in front of.

The bar's outdoor speaker system is playing an old Gerry Rafferty song, the saxophone filling the air and din of happy hour drinkers and it reminds me of my dad. I need to call him this evening to tell him the good news. One of the tour dates is in Charleston, and I know he'd make the hour and a half drive to come out. Hell, I'm even willing to send a car for him, give him the VIP treatment for an evening. God knows he needs it.

I check my phone for what seems like the hundredth time. Nicole still hasn't responded. I want her to come celebrate this win with us. She's as much responsible for this as we are. If it weren't for her, I wouldn't have written this album. Though I was able to hide my anxieties behind those first few shows that we played, I know that I couldn't have kept it up. But meeting her, being around her, it awakened something in me and the valves opened up. The words poured out onto the pages of that leather notebook that we worked in together.

That notebook that MacKenzie gave me.

I wish it had been from Nicole. I would give it back, filled with all our songs, something to keep forever. I realize in that moment, that I want to keep her forever, that I want us to be together.

When she gets here, I'm going to ask her to move in with me, to make our relationship official.

"What are you grinning about, dumbass?" Clay says, shouldering me. My beer slips and nearly spills on the table, but I'm able to catch it before it falls over.

"Hey, watch it," I say. "And I'm just excited about the tour."

"Nope," Clay shakes his head. "That's the look of something else."

"I know what it is," Chris says, taking a long draw from his beer bottle. "This dude is in love."

"I don't know what you're talking about." I avert my eyes with a sip from my bottle.

"You're constantly looking at your phone, you keep looking over your shoulder. You're in love and you're hoping she will show up at any moment," Chris continues. "To congratulate us."

I look to Dave for some support, but he just shrugs his shoulders. "Don't look at me, bro," he says. "We all see it."

"Okay, okay," I say. "Yes, I really like her. We got to spend a lot of time together lately. And yeah, I'm hoping she's going to show up and hang out with us."

Chris points and laughs. "I told you guys! I told you that he's in love with her!"

"No, I'm not," I say, but it's not very convincing.

"Man, we all saw it at the baseball game. When she showed up, you were all doe-eyed," Clay says. "But we can't blame you. Who wouldn't be in love with the hottest country star in Nashville?"

I look up in confusion. "Wait. You guys think I'm in love with…" I pause, "with MacKenzie Taylor?"

"Yes!" Chris says, nearly screaming. A few women at a table close to us turn to see what all the commotion is about.

"Whoa, whoa, whoa," I say, holding my hands up. "No way, guys."

"I mean," Dave says, "we don't blame you. Hell, we

wish she'd look at the rest of us the way she looks at you."

I look to Clay for some backup here. Surely he doesn't think that as well.

"Don't look at me, dude," he says, his eyebrows arched. "The evidence is all there. She sent you that notebook, she was all over you at the baseball game."

"Wouldn't that mean that she's the one that's into me?" I ask, pleading my case. I'd never so much as met MacKenzie Taylor before that night at the Nashville Sounds game. Sure, we'd pass each other at the Giant Records offices, and we'd done a couple of charity things together last year when the pandemic hit, but I've never actually talked with her at any length, which is why this whole thing is completely out of left field.

Besides, I've spent so much time with Nicole after the baseball game, that it felt like it'd been weeks ago, not just a few days. She's all I can ever think about. When we're not together, all I want is to be back in her presence. It's like waiting for a warm day after a cold front blows through. All you want is sunshine and warmth. That's what she is.

"You have it all wrong, all three of you," I say. "I'm in love with Nico."

The words coming out of my mouth are as much a surprise to me as it apparently is to my bandmates. Their faces are all in various contortions of shock. Even myself, I haven't admitted that out loud or even to myself until this moment, but that's exactly what this is. I'm in love with Nicole.

"Whoa," Clay finally says. "That's…that's a big deal, man."

"Yeah," Chris says. He pops open another twist-top on a beer and guzzles it down. "That's pretty heavy. What does that mean for you, and for her? Are you guys, like, officially a thing or what?"

"We haven't had that conversation yet," I say, my confidence bolstered by my outward acknowledgement of my feelings for Nicole. "But I'm going to tell her today." I feel like I can take on the world, take on anything.

"Well," Clay says. He lifts his beer in the air. "To Rett, who's finally fallen down the hole!"

We all clink bottles again, and I drink mine with gusto. I am in love with Nicole, and it feels so good to acknowledge it. I finish my bottle and place it neck-down in the metal bucket on the table. I stand up, wobbly but confident.

"I'm going to go tell her," I say. "I'm going to go tell Nico that I'm in love with her, right now."

I reach out and all the guys fist-bump and high five me. My heart is racing and all I can think about is holding her in my arms. "You've got the expense card, right?" I ask Clay.

He nods and gives me a salute. "I'll take care of it," he says.

Instead of leaving through the gate by the restaurant's entrance, I hop the metal barrier and land on the sidewalk on the other side. I pull out my phone from my back pocket and open up Uber.

"Rett." I hear my name called out and my head jerks up to the sound. Nicole is walking up the sidewalk toward me. I'm grinning ear to ear.

"Hey!" I say, my arms held out to embrace her, but she doesn't step into them. "What's wrong?" I ask.

"Look, I know you guys are having a good time over here, and I want you to know that I'm really, really happy that you guys are going on tour. I think that's incredible. But, I think we should…"

My brain is losing track of where she's going with this. My heart is racing in the opposite direction it was going in just minutes ago. *We should what?*

She takes a breath and exhales, averting her eyes and looking at the ground.

"We should what?" finally comes out of my mouth sharper than I intended it to. My mouth is suddenly dry, like I've not had anything to drink in days. "We should what, Nicole?" My tone is defensive.

"I mean, I know we haven't even had the conversation, and we're not officially in a relationship, but I just think it's time that we just called –"

I cut her off. "Don't do this. Please. Whatever is going on, it's okay. It's just a few weeks and I'll be back and we'll be back to normal. I'm in love with you."

Those five words blurt out of my dry mouth like vomit, like I'm trying to use them to desperately smother whatever she's trying to say because I know what she's trying to say.

"No you're not. Don't say that." Her tone is now angered instead of unsure.

"You don't get to tell me how I feel," I say. "Of course I am! How could I not be?"

"Look, you're about to go on tour, and that's a part of your life that I can't be in, that I don't want to be in. I don't want to spend every single day wondering and worried what you're doing, who you're with. It just doesn't work, and that's not how I want to live. You can understand that, can't you?"

"You wouldn't have to worry about anything. When have I ever given you a reason to worry? Nicole, I'm in love with you, and that doesn't change if I'm here or playing shows in God-knows-where," I say. An idea hits me. "You could come with us!"

I can't believe we're having this conversation on the sidewalk in downtown Nashville. I can sense the eyes of strangers on us, suddenly aware and entertained by our personal drama. My neck goes hot with nerves.

"No. I can't, Rett, and you know that. This assignment, this job, was temporary. I never had any desire to stay in Nashville," she says.

"What does that even mean? Why would you sleep with me? Why would you stay with me, if you knew you were just going to up and leave at any minute?" My own tone has grown angered, and I'm trying my hardest to keep my voice down. "I am in love with you. Do you understand what those words mean to me, to say them to you? So, what am I to you? Just some job? A paycheck.

The byproduct of your work?"

I am hyper-aware of the people around us. My head turns to a guy staring at us, his phone pointed our way.

"Hey," I snap at him. "You want to keep fucking walking?"

"Rett!" Nicole says.

"No," I turn back to her. "I'm not going to do this with you. You want to walk away from us, that's fine. I guess we never were really together in the first place."

I turn back to the restaurant where my bandmates are standing on the sidewalk behind us. Clay's got a look of concern, and both Chris and Dave are glaring darts at Nicole. These guys, I know, have my back no matter what.

I leave Nicole standing on the sidewalk by herself. If all I was to her was some temporary fling, then I'm not going to waste my heart and effort on her.

"Come on," Clay says as I reach them. "Let's get out of here."

CHAPTER TWENTY-FOUR

Nico

.

Rett's been gone for four weeks. The tour is nearly over. The first show was at Vanderbilt University's arena, and they played to a sold-out crowd. I only know this because of the small blurb on the newspaper's website the following Sunday. As I sit here at my writing desk, the window beside me open to the sounds of downtown Nashville below, I can't help but read a review of the tour, reading about the sold-out crowd on the most recent show of the highly-anticipated tour. My stomach turns though when I see a picture of Rett and MacKenzie together, a small rectangle set in the paragraphs. It's a candid shot, and they're looking off-stage, laughing at something. Rett looks amazing, of course. His long hair, dirty blonde and frizzed from days on the road, was tucked behind his ears, and his beard was cut close. Even in the low resolution of the photograph, his green eyes were catching.

I close the window on my laptop and open a new tab to my email. I haven't heard back yet from the University of Montana, but I obsessively check my email multiple times a day. With Rett gone and my time freed up, I find myself restless. The night he turned his back and walked away from me still runs through my mind on a loop, and I have to actively push it away. I remind myself that it was the right decision, that our lives just aren't compatible. Even if you care about someone, sometimes, your lives don't fit.

I've spent this time repairing my friendship with Gabriela. We've been out to eat together nearly every evening, or we've gone to get takeout and bring it home, sitting on the couch and binging Netflix serial killer documentaries. She's been working a lot more recently as well, and it's been nice to see her glowing and alive in her element. I can hear her right now getting ready for a commercial shoot, the blow dryer in the bathroom droning below the Snow Patrol that I've got on in my bedroom.

I realize just how involved with Rett I was, and even though he meant well, I think I simply let myself get overwhelmed with him. That made me lose sight of everything else going on around me, including my best friend.

My email dings with a notification. Every time this has happened since Rett left, my heart skips a beat. I'm at first let down that it's not a response from the University, but my head perks up as my eyes read the subject line. I read it a couple of times, my brain unable to comprehend exactly what it says.

"Gab!" I cry out. I don't think she can hear me over the blow dryer so I yell louder.

"Gabriela! I need you!"

I hear her footsteps pounding the carpet and she comes into my bedroom, the door swinging open with dramatic force. She's in a floral print silk robe and she's got a Birkenstock in one hand. Her eyes are wild, scanning the room.

"What's wrong?" she says. "Where's the spider?"

I'm turned in my chair, and I can't help but laugh, which is probably good. I need something to ease the nervousness I'm feeling.

"There's no spider," I say.

"Then why are you hollering for me like that? That sounded like a spider call."

"No, but I want you to come read this with me," I say, pointing to my open laptop screen.

"Oh!" she exclaims. "Is it the University? Did you get the job?"

"No, it's not that," I say. "But you will probably want to read this too."

Gabriela comes into the room and leans over my desk on the side that faces the bed. She squints at the screen as I open the email.

We both read it silently, unable to speak.

Gabriela has sunk onto my bed, her shoulders slumped and head low. I see tears starting to coalesce in her eyes and my own stomach turns.

It's a news article about Max Van Hope. I turn back to the screen and read it again, this time letting myself digest all of it.

An anonymous source came forward and accused him of sexual assault. When the woman no longer continued the relationship, she says that he stalked her and made her life hell, to the point that she was no longer able to find work in their industry.

"Is this –" I start, turning back to Gabriela. "Is this you?"

"No," she says, shaking her head.

I nod. "I know you don't want to. I know it was months ago and you've moved past it, but you have to come forward with your story. You have to get ahold of this attorney and tell them what Max did to you. There's no telling who else he's done this to."

"What good would it do, though?" she finally says. "Like you said, it was months ago. At this point it's just my word against his. If I were to come forward, I really would never find another job in this industry again. I already worked so hard to get back to where I was before. I don't know if I want to go through all that again, Nic."

"I know it's scary, but I'm here for you. And I know all the girls that work with you will be too. You have to come forward."

"Like you did?" she says, and the question stings. I want to lash out.

"No. Because I didn't. I tucked my tail and ran away.

But I don't want to hide anymore, and I don't want you to live like that either," I say. "Running only gets you back to where you started."

"I'm sorry," she says after a heartbeat of silence. "That was unfair of me."

"I know that I'm part of the problem. Instead of coming forward, facing what that guy did to me, I've had to silently think about it nearly every day." Tears are streaming down my face now. "I regret looking for a place to hide. I didn't need to hide. I needed to heal. And the only way to do that is to confront the trauma."

Gabriela is crying now too and she reaches out for me, her long lanky arms wrapping around me as she leans over the side of the bed. She buries her face into my neck and I stroke her hair, softly running my hands over it. I hate how much this world has taken from us, and we've been expected to be quiet about it.

Feeling Gabriela's frail frame in my arms, I can see how much it's eaten at her, chipping away bits of her happiness with guilty, knowing teeth.

I know this because it's a reflection of my own feelings.

"It's going to be okay," I say. "You're strong. You're so strong. You can do this. And I'm right here beside you. I'm going to make an official complaint with the university in Texas."

She pulls away from me and swipes at her eyes with the backs of her palms, dabbing the soft part beneath her eyelids with her bent knuckles.

"You will?"

"Yes. I will make the call today."

I can't believe that I'm going to do this, but a dam inside me breaks open and all I want to do is watch the current world succumb to the flood. It's not necessarily anger, it's just an understanding that these things can't continue to happen to us, to the women of the world. Maybe not staying silent will give other women the courage to share their stories too.

CHAPTER TWENTY-FIVE

Rett

As the giant machine slows down, I don't even know what city I'm in. The bus turns into some parking lot and I can hear the squeaking and squealing of the brakes below us. I peer out the window to get a bearing on where we're playing tonight.

This whole tour has been like this, on the go, and we're only three — no, four — weeks into it. That brings me some internal relief. We're almost done.

Every single day, we pull into some city, not even staying long enough to know its name. We run soundcheck and then get a few hours to rest before we go on stage for the night. We're out of there before the end of the show, on the bus and off to the next stop, before Mac-Kenzie has even played her encore.

We haven't even really enjoyed all the perks of our

tour bus. The concert promoter rented us a bus that I can't believe we're touring in. It's got a shower, multiple beds, a common area with a TV, and an Xbox. We even have WiFi for watching Netflix. Clay has brought his MacBook Pro and the ProTools equipment, but we haven't had time to crack into any of it; it all sits dejected in his bunk.

The crowds, though. Every single night, hearing that crush and swell of cheers reverberate through the arenas, seeing the lights of the stage, it's bigger than anything I could've ever imagined for us. Of course, I've always seen myself on a stage like that, but even in my own dreams, I had no idea how big it all would feel.

Clay rustles awake on the bench beside me and removes his sunglasses from his face. "Where are we?" he asks.

"I was about to ask you the same thing." I peer out the window of the tour bus and see the arena we're playing in tonight. It's a red-brick circular building and a sign in front reads "Reed Green Coliseum." I see the emblem of the University of Southern Mississippi on the sign.

"We're in Hattiesburg," I say.

The bus comes to a stop in the parking lot next to a couple of other buses that have MacKenzie's face plastered on the side. They belong to the tour crew, who come ahead of us to set up the stage and the lighting.

Dave opens the curtain that separates the bunks from the common area. He's got a green smoothie in his hands. "Good morning, ladies," he says. "You both look like ass."

I flip him off and rest against the cushion behind my head.

"You two seriously need to drink more water. And I don't mean Keystone, I mean actual H-two-O," he says.

I can't remember the last time I drank an actual bottle of water. There's a stocked fridge in the kitchenette of the bus, and I pull myself off the padded bench that's supposed to be a couch and shuffle that way. My head is pounding too.

I open the fridge, which is a thin, pared-down version of a regular fridge, not much larger than the one Clay and I had in our apartment in Murfreesboro when we were in college. There's all the beer – or what's left of it – and in the door, bottles of water. I grab one, twist off the top and take a greedy gulp. It feels like icepicks traveling down my throat, and it briefly masks the pain and throbbing in my temples.

"Here you go," Dave says behind me.

I turn and he's got his hand outstretched, two blue and red Tylenol pills in his palm. I pinch at them and shove them to the back of my tongue and take another swig from the water bottle. I finish it off, all sixteen ounces, in two quick gulps.

"You alright?" Dave asks, his voice low. "You look like you don't feel well."

"I'm okay, just a little hungover," I say.

It's an excuse, but a shitty one, and even I know that. We've powered through drunken nights and hangovers so many times that we're practically pros at it. Well, the three of us. Dave has always been straight-edge, vowing off alcohol, drugs. Hell, even sex. The guy is essentially a monk, and there are parts of his lifestyle I definitely envy. He wakes up early every single day, reads his Stoic devotional, and sits with his thoughts before he does anything else. There's an intentionality with the way he carries himself and the way he lives everyday life. At one time, I scoffed at his routine. I found it ridiculous, inflexible, even pretentious.

Now, I wish I had just a little bit of that commitment and focus. My mind has been going in every direction ever since we started this tour, and I just want it all to slow down.

"Nah," he says. "This isn't just a hangover. You're unbalanced. Unfocused. Ever since you and Nico broke up."

I can't argue with him. I just lean against the door of the fridge and nod.

"That's okay," he says.

I turn to look at him.

"I thought you were going to give me some hippie speech about how I should let go of my feelings and shit."

"Nah," he repeats. "Pain is good. As much as pleasure teaches us what we like, pain teaches us what we don't."

"There's the mumbo-jumbo," I say with a slight smile.

He returns it. "Breakups suck."

"Yeah," I say. "Especially the unofficial breakups. It's like, why am I sad over something that never was?"

"Because you are mourning for what could've been. You had an idea in your head and a feeling in your heart, and it was ripped away before it even had a chance to coalesce into what you wanted it to be."

"Jesus, Dave. You should be a shrink."

"That takes more education than I care for," he says, smirking. "Anyway, man, we've got to get ready for breakfast soundcheck so get your shit in order, get your head on straight and let's show Mississippi who the real star of this tour is."

He gives me a hard smack on the shoulder that shakes me awake and walks off toward the front of the bus. I notice he's barefoot. Always barefoot. Jeans, plaid button-up, but never shoes.

I grab another bottle of water from the fridge before I go back to the rear of the bus to gather my things and take a quick shower before soundcheck. There's almost always a spread of breakfast items waiting for us backstage too. Bagels, English muffins, cream cheese, sausages, the whole nine yards. Between that and the spread at night – and then the beer afterward – I'm starting to get self-conscious of my figure. I wake up feeling bloated and sore. I should probably start joining Dave for his early morning yoga.

The hot water doesn't last very long on the bus, but I'm able to get washed and shave my neck. It does make my head feel better, though. I feel like I can function and sing.

Our soundcheck runs first, and we usually wrap up by

eleven, in time for a quick lunch and rest up before that evening's show. On nights that we don't have to travel more than four hundred miles, like tonight, we get a hotel. After lunch we'll get to check in and relax for a bit. I am looking forward to a real bed.

After about twenty minutes, I throw on a t-shirt and a pair of jeans and walk in through the back doors of the venue. I can already hear music blaring from the arena's sound system, and the bass reverberates through my chest. As I get to the stage, I pull my in-ear monitors on, and check for the sound in them. They're already connected to the sound system and I give a thumbs-up to the guy at the board.

My Telecaster is on a black stand beside the stage and I take it in my hands, strumming a few chords to make sure it's on and connected as well.

"Alright," I say into the microphone at the front of the stage. "Let us know when you're ready."

The sound guy in the booth in the middle of the cavernous, empty arena gives me a thumbs-up and I turn to my band. Chris, behind the drumkit, counts us off and we play the first song. I lean into the microphone.

"I need a bit more bass in my mix, please," I say. I hear the bass come forward through my monitors and I nod. "That's good."

It goes like this for about an hour and a half. We get the sound right for the venue and then play through our set. Then, we work on the new material for about thirty minutes before we have to tear down and let MacKenzie's band prepare for their own soundcheck.

The new songs are sounding incredibly tight. I've given instructions to the soundboard operator to record every soundcheck to a USB drive. The guys and I will spend a few hours in the afternoon listening to it, making notes for adjustments and tweaks. By the time we get back to Nashville, we'll be able to get in our studio and know exactly what to do.

As we finish up our setlist, I hear a faint applause out in the seats. Squinting through the shine of the stage lights, I peer down into the cavern of the auditorium and see MacKenzie down there. She's in a hoodie and sunglasses with a sweating cup of iced coffee clutched in one hand.

"Was that some of the new material?" she shouts from below, her voice echoing through the arena.

I nod. "Yeah. Come on up."

She snakes her way through the emptiness and makes it up to the stage.

"The new stuff is sounding so good, y'all," she says. She stands too close to me and I intentionally take a step back. She takes another step forward and I relent.

"Thanks," Chris says from behind the drum kit, but MacKenzie pays him no mind, turning to me like he hadn't said a word.

"Have you seen this?" she asks, shoving a cell phone up to my face. I have to lean back to let my eyes focus on the screen.

The web browser is open to a website, and there's a picture of me, guitar slung over my shoulder, my lips contorted in a strange way as I am playing some riff. The headline above the image reads *Rett Gordon, Preparing for Second Album, Wowing Audiences on MacKenzie Taylor Tour.*

"Wowing?" I ask, more to myself than anyone else.

"You're a star, baby." MacKenzie smiles, looking up at me. If it were Nicole, I would take her up in my arms and kiss her. But she's not Nicole, and her Cheshire cat grin sends shivers down my spine more than it warms my heart.

"I don't know about that," I say, my voice cracking and fragile.

"So, I was thinking about something," she says, again disregarding anyone else. "We should do a duet!"

My lips purse. "I don't know," I start, but MacKenzie cuts me off.

"Oh, come on!" she implores. "It would be huge for us and for the tour. We'll do it in my encore. Just imagine being splashed all over Rolling Stone before your next album comes out."

That does sound pretty damn enticing, to be featured in some of the larger music magazines and websites the way that MacKenzie is. Despite what she says, it's clear that she's the real star.

But, I'm suspicious of her motivations here.

"That sounds great," I say. I give the guys a side-eye glance, to get a feel for their unspoken collective opinion. Their eyes tell me exactly what they're thinking. "But, we're usually out of here by the time you go on for your encore."

"But not tonight, right? You guys are staying at the hotel tonight? Problem solved."

I purse my lips again. It's obvious that she's thought this through.

"Are you sure you want to share the stage together?" I ask. "I mean, we're just the supporting act."

"Of course I do. It will be good publicity for both of us." She looks at the band and corrects herself. "All of us."

"Well, let me think about it," I say. "We'd have to run through a whole soundcheck and rehearse it before I'd be comfortable saying yes. Besides, we'd have to learn to sing a song together."

"Oh, duh," she says. "I wouldn't just throw you out there. Why don't you guys go get some lunch and then you come back to meet me here afterward? We'll do 'Lights All Around'."

The song was one of the new ones from her latest record, with a pop-like beat. It's something outside of my comfort zone, but it's a catchy track.

Again, I look at Clay. He gives me a slight shrug as if to say, *couldn't hurt to try.*

"Okay," I say, turning back to MacKenzie. "I'm not saying I'll do it, but I'll come back after lunch and we can workshop it."

She launches herself at me and wraps her arms around my neck. I have to steady myself from being toppled over by her enthusiasm.

"This is going to be great!" She nearly squeals in excitement. "Okay," she says, letting go of me. I smooth out my shirt that's been hiked up over my belt. "I'll let you guys finish and then I'll see you this afternoon."

MacKenzie twirls and exits the stage. I grab my guitar from the rack on the stage and pull it over my shoulders, checking the strap locks.

"Damn," Chris says. "I don't think she even realizes there are three other guys in this band."

I wave him off. "Don't worry about it. She's just after the paparazzi. Has to stay in the spotlight."

"Whatever you say, man," he says.

I strum my guitar, and its treble timbre reverberates through the arena. I say into the microphone, "Let's run through the first song again, just so it's crisp."

The sound guy in the booth at the back of the arena gives me a thumbs up and Chris counts us off. We play through the song flawlessly, but I don't hear a single word of it. My mind is elsewhere.

CHAPTER TWENTY-SIX

Nico

The office feels sterile, cold, as I hold Gabriela's hand. She tells the attorney what happened to her with Max Van Hope, the parts that she remembers. It's so heartbreaking to hear her tell her story through sobs. I don't even realize I'm holding my breath. The woman on the other side of the mahogany desk listens and lets Gabriela speak until there's nothing left for her to say. I had no idea how painful the tubal pregnancy and the emotional aftermath was for my closest friend.

The attorney's office is in one of the high rises downtown, and through the large plate glass windows, I can see the bustle of life below. It makes me think of all the lives being lived there, right now, and I find myself wishing for Rett. Wishing that he was here with us, holding my hand. I remember being at the hospital when we still didn't know what was going on, and he was right there, supportive and doing everything he could to be there for me.

"Gabriela, you are so brave to come forward and talk to me. I have a few questions I need to ask, if you're comfortable with that?" the attorney, Susan Clark, says.

She nods her head, in agreement. I had her a tissue.

"I need you to be very specific about the details you do remember. Can you walk me through what you were doing there and when you met up with Max Van Hope?"

"From what I remember," Gabriela says, "we were at the afterparty at a private bar downtown. It's in a loft building close to the Van Hope Group offices. It's a big get-together with all the models and the sponsors. Max usually doesn't come to these things, but he was there that night. I remember thinking that was weird, because he'd asked me earlier that evening if I was going to be there. Anyway, he shows up, and almost makes a beeline for me. Like, he was there to see me. Of course, I was flattered, maybe even a little excited, which makes me sick to admit. I mean, this was huge. He's the president of the company. If he's noticed me, I thought, it could mean a lot for my career."

"Did he come onto you right away, or make you feel uncomfortable in any way at first?"

"No," Gabriela answers, almost guiltily. "He was very courteous, charming, even. Asked me how I liked being with the Van Hope Group, asked me about coming to Nashville, all that stuff. He seemed genuinely interested in me."

The attorney makes notes as Gabriela talks, occasionally nodding her head or giving an "mmmhmmm."

Gabriela continues, "Some of the other girls would come up and talk to me, but I think they were trying to get his attention as well. It was clear that he was giving me all of his focus. Of course it made me feel special, in the moment. I," she chokes on her words and I squeeze her hand, "I liked the attention."

"That's a natural response," the attorney says. "There's no shame in that. We all like attention from people, especially positive attention that we think can help further our careers. It's intrinsically important. So, the party is happening, there are a lot of people around. When did you find yourself alone with Mr. Van Hope?"

"That's the thing," Gabriela says. "I don't remember ever going off alone together. It wasn't like a high school party where you go upstairs to the bedrooms or anything. At one point, he offered to grab a couple of drinks for us from the bar."

"Uh huh," the attorney says, again scribbling notes. "And you didn't go with him? To the bar?"

"No. He left me as he went to order our drinks, and I continued to talk with some of the other girls there. He came back a few minutes later. Gin and tonic for me. Some kind of whiskey for him."

"Did you have any inclination that he would have spiked your drink with some sort of impairing drug?"

"Not at the time, no," Gabriela says. "I trusted him,

you know? He was president of the company, not some random guy out on Broadway on a Saturday night. I trusted him completely."

"What happened after that? You start drinking together?"

"That's the thing. It gets pretty hazy after that. I felt like the alcohol hit me pretty hard, and I was having a difficult time focusing. That's all I remember until I woke up the next morning, without my clothes on. In the bed next to him."

I sit there in silence, squeezing Gabriela's hand, thinking back on my own experience. It wasn't the president of the company. But it was so similar. The alcohol, the attention. The man in a position of power above me. We had gone out together. Everything seemed fine until it wasn't. Until I woke up in his bed with no recollection of the night before and a pain between my thighs.

The only difference was, I didn't end up with a pregnancy that left me in the hospital afterward. But the scars still remain.

CHAPTER TWENTY-SEVEN

Rett

I've never heard a crowd that loud in my entire life, much less my career. Even when I saw U2 back in college, there wasn't this kind of response, despite me screaming my head off. Here, those screams are aimed at me. Well, at the stage, and at MacKenzie, who is shining in the spotlight.

She holds the microphone up to her lips. "You want more?"

The crowd screams in response, deafening again.

"We're going to do something special tonight, just for you," she says.

I had spent the entirety of her set backstage, waiting for this, growing more and more nervous as her band played. We rehearsed this afternoon, running soundchecks, getting the harmonies correct. It's one of her songs, one of the singles from her last album, and it works well for a duet, but I'm envious of my bandmates who have already left for the hotel. I'm sure they're already in bed, relaxing, while I'm still on this stage, sweating my ass off.

The crowd screams again and the band starts the song. MacKenzie walks across the stage toward me.

"What do you think of this guy?" she asks the crowd and the response is shrill, thousands of females screaming at the top of their lungs. MacKenzie puts her arm around my shoulder, and my hand almost involuntarily slips around her waist.

"You ready to give them a show?" she asks.

I hold my microphone up. Usually, all my nervousness melts away when I perform, but that's not happening now. I can feel the tremble in my throat before I even sing. I can hide any nervousness behind a guitar when I perform, but now, in front of this screaming crowd, I feel naked. I do my best to push it away, to focus on the song, on all the rehearsing we did this afternoon.

MacKenzie sings the first lines of the verse, and I follow up with the second part. I can hear it in my monitors that I'm flat, my voice is shaky. She gives me an encouraging look and I resolve myself to get back in key. With the second line, our voices do harmonize, and as we sing together it's clear the crowd loves it. By the time we finish the duet, my nervousness has been replaced with excitement and energy.

It's hard to believe that just a few months ago, we

were playing clubs in downtown Nashville. Sure, we were getting some national attention and the attention was starting to boil to something larger, but it hadn't exploded yet. Now, in front of these arenas, I know that this is what we've been working toward.

At the same time, I wish that I was enjoying this moment with my own band.

* * *

After the show, I want to go back directly to the hotel. I know that we have to be on the road early tomorrow to get to the next show, but MacKenzie insists that I join her for a post-show drink.

We're backstage in the green room – which is much more impressive and stocked than the storage-closet-turned-dressing-room we get as the supporting act – and I can't help but be envious of the spread that she and her band get. There are tables and tables of food, ice chests full of beer and sodas. There's even a bowl of miniature chocolate bars, the wrappers haphazardly thrown in the direction of a nearby trash can. It's a completely different environment than what we are afforded.

I'm sitting on one of the couches – not a folding chair in sight – and MacKenzie brings me a red Solo cup filled from the keg that's nearly floating in a bucket of ice water. The beer is still cold as I bring it to my lips. It's good stuff, too, not the cheap shit we usually drink backstage.

"That was so good," she says. She takes a seat next to

me on the opposite end of the couch, pulling her legs up and sitting on them. She still has glitter and makeup all over her face, and it is jarring in the regular lights back here. "I think they really enjoyed that."

"Yeah. I hate that I came in flat, but I think that if –" I say, but I'm immediately cut off as MacKenzie takes her phone in her hands.

"I can't wait to see what Twitter has to say about it," she says. She scrolls through her social media feeds as I sit in silence, my thoughts and concerns about the duet having been completely ignored and cast aside.

"Ah!" she exclaims, and holds the phone out to my face. There's a shot of us on stage from the crowd with a caption: Country's hottest stars – literally! #rettgordon #MacKenzietaylor.

"I'm a hashtag?" I ask.

"Hell yeah you're a hashtag. You're so famous," she says.

I know the band has a Twitter and all the other socials, but I don't keep up with it much personally. That's generally Dave's department. Or Clay's. I couldn't care less about social media.

"That's weird. People actually post about me?"

"Oh, all the time. Here, check it out."

She hands me her phone and there's an entire #rettgordon feed. Pictures of me on stage, some press photos, even some candid photos of me walking along the street or sitting at a café. It all feels very weird. I hand the phone back to her without saying anything.

"In this industry, people want to feel like they know us, like they want to be our friends," MacKenzie says. "Showing them real life, they like it. We're approachable. Well, we seem approachable. There are the weirdos too." She laughs.

I gulp.

"Oh, it's not that bad, don't look like that. I don't think you have anything to worry about, unless you start getting weird fan mail."

"Have you gotten anything weird?" I ask.

"Oh, for sure. Granted, I have a whole team who answers my fan mail these days, but I used to open everything myself, and I would personally respond to as many as I could, until it became too much. But yeah. Once one guy sent me his boxer shorts. And I've gotten lots of dick pics. It's awful."

"Holy shit," I respond. I take a drink from the beer, and I immediately wish it was water. "Hey, can I get a bottle of water instead? I've been drinking way too much on this tour and I should really cut back."

"Oh yeah, of course." MacKenzie snaps her fingers and some guy in a black polo shirt comes over. Even though we're sitting, he still towers over us, this giant barrel of a man, the low lights reflecting off his shaved head.

"Yes ma'am?" he asks, his voice gruff.

"Bottle of water for my friend, please," she says.

He turns to me. "Sparkling or still?"

I shrug my shoulders. "Just a regular old bottle of water. Hell, tap would be fine too at this point."

MacKenzie laughs way too hard.

The guy leaves to fetch the water and I turn back to her. "Hey," I say. "Sort of on the subject. Can I ask you something?"

"Of course."

"That notebook. Why did you send it to me?"

She gives me a quizzical look. "You didn't like it?"

The gentleman in the black polo brings back a bottle of water, some expensive-looking brand, and I thank him. I twist off the cap and take a sip. It's cold, much colder than the beer from the keg. "No, yeah," I say. "It's really nice, but it was just such a surprise, you know?"

"Good. It was meant to be." She smiles again, this flirty lip-bite that makes me blush. "I knew you were starting to write the new record. I was such a fan of the first one, and I wanted to get you something that would make the album memorable, something you could look back on in twenty or thirty years and remember the process."

Even now, I think about that process, and it had nothing to do with MacKenzie Taylor. It was Nicole and me, together on Saturday mornings, making pancakes, playing guitar in my living room. Scenes and images flash through my head of those days, how perfect they were. Nicole dancing, shaking her hips to a song, wearing one of my flannels. Her perfect body wrapped in my sheets. I want so badly to go back to those days, but they're gone forever now.

Maybe, though, after this tour, I can call her up. We

can talk about everything.

I miss her.

"What's wrong?" MacKenzie asks, and I snap out of my memories.

"Oh, nothing. But, yeah, thank you," I say. "For the lyric book. It was, um, it was …" I trail off, distracted as I notice that MacKenzie has scooted closer to me on the couch.

"You're very welcome. Anything I can do to help, I'm here for you." Again, she moves closer, her free arm up on the back cushion as she takes a drink.

"I appreciate that," I say. "I think I better head back to the hotel. My bandmates are waiting for me."

"You don't want to hang out a little longer? I was thinking about grabbing something to eat before going back to the hotel as well." She again glides closer, somehow moving without moving, almost hovering, and she's nearly in my lap at this point.

"Yeah, I'm sure. We have an early soundcheck, you know?" I say.

"Not tomorrow you don't." Her response is full of trouble.

"Right, we have to be up early to get to the next city." I smile, and stand from the couch. I finish off the bottle of water, and an attendant comes over to take the empty from my hand before I can even find the trash can.

"Another, sir?" the guy asks. His politeness is unnerving.

"No, I'm good, thank you. On my way out," I say.

Turning back to MacKenzie, who is staring up at me with her emerald-green eyes, giving me the look that I've seen from countless women in the pit in front of the stage, that look that says, *say the word and I'm yours.* I give her a courteous nod.

"Thank you," I say. "For everything. For the notebook, the opportunity for this tour, for it all."

"You're too sweet," she says. She stands and wraps her arms around my waist. Her head tilts up and she kisses me on the cheek. "Let's do this again soon."

"Okay," I say, almost instinctively. The fact of the matter is, her attention is unwelcome. It's not comfortable the way Nicole's touch is comforting. The way Nicole rests her head on my chest, our legs tangled in sheets after waking up from a short night. I miss her so much, and MacKenzie's attention amplifies that, amplifies the way that I can't feel comfortable having another woman that close to me.

"Goodnight," she says.

"Goodnight."

With the help of one of the venue guys, I find my way out of the arena into the much needed night air. Mississippi nights are warm and salty, the ocean breeze blowing in. The hotel is a ten-minute walk, and it takes me that long to clear my mind, to tuck the part of me that misses Nicole back into its compartment.

CHAPTER TWENTY-EIGHT

Nico

I want to throw up. I don't even read the caption above the Instagram post. All I see is a candid shot of Rett canoodling on some backstage couch with MacKenzie Taylor. That's probably why he agreed to this tour in the first place. I don't even want to click on the picture to read the *Daily Nashville* gossip piece, but my fingers defy my instructions, as do my eyes.

Are country music darlings MacKenzie Taylor and Rett Gordon Dating? it reads.

I feel my stomach drop, making me queasy. "Ugh," I say, out loud.

"What?" Gabriela asks.

She's sitting across the table from me in the midday sunlight. It's a gorgeous late-summer afternoon and she's glowing in a way that I haven't seen in a long time. She looks…happy. Like a weight has been lifted off her shoulders and she can hold her head up once again. She's picking at a garden salad with her fork, fishing out the bits of onion. "I always tell them no onion, but here I am, a bowl full of onions," she whines. "Anyway, what are you *ugh*-ing about?"

I turn the phone and show her the screen. She shoves some salad in her mouth and chews contemplatively. "Well," she says. "What did you think was going to happen? You dumped him on a sidewalk. Now he's on tour with the hottest girl in music. I'm surprised it didn't happen sooner. They're, what, a month into the tour?"

"Thanks for making me feel better," I say, sarcastically. "I just didn't think I'd see it plastered all over my newsfeed, you know? It's not like dating some regular guy. When you break up and you run into him at the grocery store four months later and he's got some graduate assistant hanging on his arm and a basket full of organic vegetables and oat milk."

"That's oddly specific." Gabriela tilts her head inquisitively.

"Yes, well, instead, I get to see his romance with this pop star play out in real time. It'll be all over Facebook, all over the gossip mags. The only way to avoid it will be to shut my eyes and only watch re-runs of The Office." I take a bite from one of my tacos and chew with indignance.

"You broke up with him, remember? This was your choice."

"Yes, I recall."

"So? What are you upset about?"

"I mean, I didn't come to Nashville to fall in love, but he and I became really close. And I think maybe I pushed him away because I was having such—"

She cuts me off. "So you're in love with him?" Her eyebrows raise.

"I didn't say that."

"Um, yes you did."

"When?"

"Just now. You said that you didn't come out here to fall in love. But you did. You did fall in love. You're in love with him," she says.

"No, that's not what I meant." I pause. Actually, that's exactly what I meant. Whether I want to admit it or not, I was – I am – in love with Rett Gordon. But I wasn't ready to admit that to myself. I wasn't ready to face those feelings because I was still reeling from everything that happened in Texas.

"Look, I know what you were running from. Trust me, I do. And when something good would come along, you'd run from that too, because you hadn't confronted your own problems. You hadn't solved them. But it's different now. You've dealt with what happened and you're healing. We both are. And now we're seeing the trail of things we ran away from in our rearview. You've also made this decision to go back to Missoula. So, I guess I'm wondering what you are running from now? From him? From love? What happens after that? When are you going to look back and realize that everything you wanted, you left in the dust?"

Wow. That hurts. Not because it's mean. Because it's true. And it's on the table now, as real as Gabbi's empty salad bowl, staring me in the face.

As if she can read my mind, Gabriela continues, "I know that sounds mean, but I hope you don't think that. I hope you don't think I'm being mean to you. But this is what you do, Nic. You run away, you start over. You *change your name*. But it doesn't change anything. You're still you. And you still have to deal with you at the end of the day."

My taco drops on the plate. I can feel the tears well up, so I grab the napkin beneath my margarita and dab the corners of my eyes with it. Gabriela reaches across the table to take my hand and she gives it a maternal squeeze.

"You've got to stop running," she says.

"I know," I answer. "But, it doesn't really matter anyway, I don't think he loves me back. At least not anymore. I embarrassed him in public."

"So you are in love with him?" she asks again.

I let the truth of what I just said occupy the space between us. I am, very much so. I just couldn't allow myself to admit it before, because the broken parts hurt too much. I was so scared that I wouldn't even allow myself the chance to love or be loved. Flashes of memories come rushing back. All those times that Rett was there for me and taking care of me. He'd make a cup of coffee for me in the morning. I don't even think he knew how much that simple gesture meant. And then, the way he'd look at me while cooking breakfast or how he held my hand on the way back from South Carolina. All those little moments when rolled up, were much bigger than the sum of their parts. They made me feel safe, showed me how much he cared, and right now they're showing me how much I always wanted to be with him.

"I think I screwed this one up," I say. "He's out on tour now and MacKenzie Taylor has her claws in him. I'm maybe too late."

"That's just some celebrity gossip mag hogwash," she says. "You know the truth."

I nod again. The truth is, if he feels the same way about me as I feel about him, then it doesn't matter where he's on tour or who he's with. That part of his career isn't going away, and I can't get caught up on what the gossip blogs say. At the end of the day, they have to sell pictures and get views and clicks.

"What should I do? Just go find him on whatever tour stop he's on right now and tell him that I'm in love with him?" I ask.

"Yes."

I laugh at her one-word answer. "You're so helpful, you know that?" And she really is.

"Look, you held my hand through the hardest thing I've ever experienced in my life. I wanted to die. But, you were right there the entire time, Nic. You are my best friend. So now I'm going to hold your hand through this, kick your ass in gear a little, and I'm not gonna let you run away again," she says.

"Okay." I smile.

"Now, where is he on tour this week?"

I pull out my phone and we check out the tour dates. The shows are mostly regional; the furthest they're going is Tulsa.

"Looks like they're in Baton Rouge tomorrow night," I say.

"How far is that?"

"I don't know." I calculate the distance. "About eight, nine hours from here."

"Road trip?" her face is suddenly mischievous, a look in her eye that I haven't seen since we were in college.

"Pack your bags," I say, returning her grin.

CHAPTER TWENTY-NINE

Rett

The tour is almost done, and I've never missed my own bed so much in my life. I walk through the bunks to the middle area of the bus. Clay's got on a pair of headphones that are plugged into his laptop. He doesn't even see me come into the common area. His face is cradled in his hands and his eyes are full of concentration.

I haven't had a beer in four nights, and aside from the lower back pain that's from the incredibly uncomfortable bed mattress, I feel great. My head hasn't pounded in almost a week. I open the fridge and find a bottle of water and a yogurt.

"Hey man," Clay says as I shut the door. "I didn't even see you come in. I thought the fridge opened by itself."

"I wouldn't be surprised," I say. "The more I look at this thing, the more I think it's held together with wishes and baling wire."

I slide into the booth across from him. He pulls the headphones from around his neck and passes them over.

"Check this out," he says.

I put the headphone on and music flows through. It's one of our demo recordings, but it's been polished up and mixed. The drums sound incredible.

"This sounds really good," I say.

"The label wants it to be the first single," he says.

"I could live with that. It's a good song."

It's one that Nicole helped the most on, so of course it's good. Not only is she talented with words, but the way she was able to get the lines to match with the melody, it all came together in this total package that I could've never done on my own.

I pull the headphones off from around my neck and toss them back over.

"We'll hit the ground running when we get back to Nashville," I say. "We'll go from living in a bus to living in our studio."

"Yeah," Clay says. "But at least I can drag my own mattress to the studio."

"You too, huh?"

"Oh man. My lower back feels like it belongs to an eighty-year-old. I feel like I could hobble into a Denny's and they'd give me the senior special out of compassion."

I laugh. "I feel like we're too young for back problems."

"Pushing thirty," Clay says.

"Damn, you're right." I lean into the bench and look out the window as the highway lines zip past. I'm admittedly growing tired of this part of the tour, the roads and the bus and the terrible sleep. As much as I love the cheering and adoring fans, I feel the exact opposite about the inner workings of the tour.

"I stuck around last night, saw the encore," Clay says. I'm pulled out of my thoughts.

"Oh yeah?"

"I can see why all the gossip rags are going on and on about you two."

"Oh god," I sigh. "I never thought we'd be so big that gossip blogs would be talking about us."

"Well, to be fair, they're talking about MacKenzie. You just happen to be ancillary to it."

"Clay," I laugh. "What the hell does *ancillary* mean?"

He shakes his head in response. "I'm sorry."

That's how he's always been though. Smarter than the rest of us, working on a mental level that we'll never comprehend. His understanding of music theory and composition makes the entire band better, though, even if what he says generally goes over our heads.

He continues, "What I mean is, MacKenzie has to stay in the spotlight. It's part of the gig, part of the job of being MacKenzie Taylor. As soon as she falls out of the attention sphere, it's over for her. That's why she moved from country to pop. Sure, she still plays some of those old hits at the shows, but her latest record showed that she's reinventing because she has to."

"What about us then?" I ask. "Are we going to have to spend our entire career chasing some kind of spotlight?"

"If we're true to who we are and what we set out to do – write good music – then the spotlight will follow us."

"You seem so sure of yourself."

"My biggest fear is that we start chasing that elusive dragon. The dragon of popularity," he says.

"Instead of chasing the music?"

"Exactly."

Dave walks into the common area, stretching his lower back.

"God," he says. "I feel like I slept under the tires all night."

Clay and I both laugh. "Join the club," I say.

Dave grabs a bottled green smoothie from the fridge. I scoot over in the booth and he slides in next to me. Cracking the lid, he takes a sip and offers the bottle to me.

"Hair of the dog?" he asks.

I laugh again, take a sip and hand him back the bottle. It tastes like spinach and banana. Two flavors that, a month ago, I would have gagged at. Now, it's starting to taste good.

Well, maybe not good. But good for me.

"How many more nights of this do we have?" Dave asks.

"Four more shows. Tonight, in Baton Rouge. Then,

over to Austin, up to Waco, then Tulsa," Clay says.

"How do you even know all that?" I ask.

"How do you not?" he responds. "Gotta know where you're playing. Don't want to be in Santiago and call it San Diego you know," he says.

"True, true. It's just, I don't even know what day it is. Everything has been such a blur."

These past four weeks have gone by both like lightning and slower than I could imagine. Mostly because every free moment I have, I think of Nicole. I don't know why, though. She hasn't so much as texted me once throughout this whole month. I thought I'd at least hear from her, a courteous "good luck" text. But, nothing.

Maybe I really was just a gig to her. A job with an expiration date. Now that the album is written, she's off to the next gig, the next thing that'll pay. I should be more upset, because I feel like we had a real connection. Maybe we did.

As I'm lost in my thoughts about Nicole, Clay and Dave discuss the album and the recording plan. Chris walks in, yawning.

"Good morning, ladies," he says. "Where are we?"

"Heading to," I pause, glancing at Clay inquisitively, "Baton Rouge?"

"Baton Rouge tonight, Austin tomorrow," Clay nods.

"My ears are still ringing from last night," Chris says as he slides into the booth next to Clay. "I've never heard so many shrill voices screaming all at once."

"The encore?" I ask.

"Yeah. That duet you guys are doing is really good, and it's obvious the crowd loves it, but shit, I'm going to need hearing aids at the end of this tour," Chris says.

"I'm not going to be able to hear right for a month after we get home," I say.

I've missed hanging out like this, just the four of us. It's quiet, but it feels like it used to, back in college, when we were making music in our dorm, or when we rented a rehearsal space at a storage facility. We could just hang out without some expectation of a new record or album sales or a tour. All of those things were still just pipe dreams.

Somehow, "making it" feels a lot less glamorous than I'd envisioned back then. This feels like work. Grueling, clock-in-and-clock-out work.

"Is that the track you were working on last night?" Chris asks as he leans over to the open MacBook screen.

"Yeah, just mastering it down and then going to email it over to David at the label."

"Might want to hold off on that," Chris says. "Might not be a label by the time we get back."

All of our eyes go wide.

"What are you talking about?" I ask.

Chris looks at all of us, his eyes darting. "Wait. Seriously, you guys don't know?"

"Know what?"

"The Van Hope Group is under investigation."

"Investigation?" I ask. "For what?"

Chris pulls his phone out of his pocket, taps on the

screen and then hands the device over to me.

I immediately do a double-take. The story is brief, but it details that Max Van Hope of the Van Hope Group has stepped down from his post as Vice President of the company amid sexual assault allegations.

"Whoa," I say. "This girl that's quoted, that says she was drugged and impregnated, that's Nico's roommate. You guys remember? Back in March when I spent all night at the hospital with her?"

Chris nods as he takes the phone back.

"No wonder Nico was so distant and quick to break up. She was just dealing with a lot. God, I'm an idiot. I should've seen it. I should've been more cognizant of what was going on with that situation instead of sticking my head up my ass trying to get this record finished." I feel like I let down the woman I love by not being more aware of the things happening around her.

"Wow," Chris says, raising his eyebrows in disbelief. "You used a big boy word."

I flip him off. "Seriously. I need to call her. Tonight, after the show." I slump in the seat, feeling sorry for my-self, but Clay snaps me out of it.

"Not just that, dude," he says as he reads over the news story. "What's going to happen with the label now? What are we going to go back home to? Shit, we've got four shows left. What if the rest of the tour is cancelled?"

"I don't think they'll do that," Dave says. "They still have an obligation to the tour company and all the people who bought tickets. If there were more than four shows left, I think they'd cancel it, but we're so close to the end, they'll let us ride it out."

"This is huge though," Chris says. "The entire label image, the Van Hope Group, it's all tarnished now."

"And we're supposed to put out an album this fall," I say. Sighing, I look out the window, the scenery changing from trees and swamps to a more urban sprawl. We're approaching Baton Rouge, to play a concert for thousands of screaming fans, but all I want to do is find a hole to crawl into.

And hug Nicole.

* * *

The show tonight is as loud and raucous as the rest, but I can tell something is off, especially with MacKenzie's set. It's not until our duet in her encore – which has become both a social media and gossip blog buffet of speculation – that I see tears in her eyes, as MacKenzie powers through her last few songs.

I go backstage to the green room, and what's usually a bustling area of bodies and work to prepare for the next night, is now quiet, dark, and empty. I've got a bottle of water in my hand but the stench of booze is heavy back here.

"MacKenzie?" I call out.

"Back here," I hear her say, like a child hiding from angry parents.

"Hey." I find her sitting against the white cinderblock

wall. "Are you okay?"

She's got a bottle of booze in her hand, swirling it around before taking a swig. "I don't know."

I approach her and let my body slide against the wall and fall to the hard concrete floor. "Worried about the tour?"

She huffs. "Fuck this tour. All of this. The label. The Van Hopes. All of them."

"I take it you heard the news?" It's not that I'm surprised, but I figured things would be more hush-hush as we finished up these last shows.

"Heard the news? Rett, I *am* the news," she spits. "Sure, some models with his little side gig or whatever came forward, but you think they were the first? Hell, I doubt I was the first."

It takes me a second to comprehend what she's saying, partly due to how forced and labored her words are, the syllables sliding and slurring into one another. It's clear that she didn't just start drinking. She may have been on the bottle all day.

"Oh, MacKenzie," I finally say. "I'm so sorry. Do you want to talk about it? Is there anything I can do?"

"Unless you have a time machine to go back to 2015 and make me sign that contract with Sony instead of taking a chance on the Van Hope Group, I don't think there's much anyone can do."

I reach over to put my arm around her, to offer some sort of comfort. She's hesitant at first but leans into my shoulder. She takes another swig.

"I'm so stupid," she says.

"No you aren't."

"Yes. I should've known that this would happen. That's what this industry does. It takes girls like me and makes us do things we don't want to in the name of celebrity. In the name of making it. Well, I don't feel like I'm making it. I feel like I'm faking it. I feel like I've been faking it for six years, Rett. Six damn years that I've spent trying to make people happy. Except for me."

I take the bottle of Jack from her hand and take a sip. The alcohol burns as it goes down my throat. I haven't had a beer in nearly two weeks; hard liquor even longer. "God that stings," I say, shaking my head and letting my cheeks loosen.

"What do I do now? If I come forward, I'm damaged goods. No one is going to sign me. If I don't, I have to live with this forever. This guilt," she says. She's sobbing now, and I hold her tighter.

"What do you think is the right thing to do?"

"I don't know. I was so young. I was seventeen. He made me feel special. It started with attention, and then it became more and more, until he was on top of me. And you know what? I closed my eyes the entire time. I didn't want the image of him on me like that," she says through her tears.

"I can't even imagine," I say. I think about Nicole's roommate, nearly dying from an accidental pregnancy, and the grief and strife in the aftermath of that. I feel the heat of anger rising to my ears, the back of my neck getting warm.

"Here's what we're going to do," I say. "We're going to finish this tour. We're going to show our fans and the people in this business that you, MacKenzie Taylor, are a warrior. That nothing and no one can stop you. That this industry is dirty, but it doesn't have to be, and you can persevere despite that."

She smiles through her tears. "You're right. I can do this."

"You're damn right you can," I say.

She takes another swig from the bottle and offers it to me, but I decline. "I'm trying to cut back."

"Well," she says, pulling the bottle back, "I'm not."

We both laugh at that. I stand up and stretch my back. "I think I'm going to head back to the hotel," I say. "We've got to be on the bus early tomorrow to head to Austin."

MacKenzie looks up at me with the eyes of a puppy in a kennel, who wants to be picked up and held. It's an almost innocent frailty. "Can I," she starts, "I don't want to be alone, and I feel safe with you. Can I come with you?"

CHAPTER THIRTY

Nico

I texted Clay to get the hotel details earlier in the day, and as we pull into the Baton Rouge hotel parking lot, my hands go clammy with sweat. It's nearly midnight. We had some epic car karaoke sessions somewhere between Birmingham and Hattiesburg to keep ourselves alert and awake. I have an entire speech in my head, but what I really want is to throw my arms around Rett's neck and feel the warmth that only he provides. I know we have to talk first and I'm a nervous wreck.

Gabriela pulls the Nissan, a rental car we got early that morning, into a free parking spot. There are still people mingling on the hotel's open patio, a Bluetooth speaker somewhere pumping music. As we walk up to the main front doors, I can see some of the crowd have MacKenzie Taylor tour t-shirts on.

The hotel's automatic sliding doors open to a lobby that echoes with voices and a ringing phone. I give the desk attendant a nod and continue walking toward the bank of elevators that lead up to the sixth floor.

Inside the elevator, punching at the button, I fan myself.

"Are you going to be alright?" Gabriela asks.

"Yeah, just, you know," I say.

"I don't think I've seen you this nervous since senior prom." She gives me a knowing smile and a nudge.

"That was a disaster and you know it," I say.

"Yeah, but you still stabbed Clark with that boutonniere, your hands were shaking so bad."

"Can we talk about something else?" I ask. I fan myself with my clammy hands.

"Just breathe," she says. "It's not every day you admit your undying love to the man of your dreams."

"What?" I ask, incredulous. "Undying love? Man of my dreams? What is this, a rom-com? No, I'm just going to tell him that I was wrong and I let my own insecurities get in the way of what we have and —"

Before I can finish, the elevator dings and the doors open to a hallway that stretches out for yards in either direction. "Which room is it again?" Gabriela asks as we step out.

"610," I say. The sign mounted to the wall says that rooms 601-622 are to the left so we start that way.

The hallway is quiet, but I can hear the occasional television as we pass by a couple of the rooms. We reach

610 and I hesitate. Taking a long breath, I knock.

A few seconds later – seconds that stretched on for minutes – the door cracks open. It's Rett. He's in jeans and a white t-shirt. He sees me, realizes it's me, and his eyes go wide.

"Holy shit," he says, standing in the door. "Wow! What…" he starts. "What are you doing here?"

"I just couldn't take it anymore," I say. "I've been doing a lot of thinking and –" I pause, my attention pulled away by a shift of movement behind him.

"Who is it? Rett? Who's at the door?" a female's voice asks, the words slurred.

I peer over his shoulder and all feeling leaves my body. "You've got to be shitting me," I say. "This was a mistake."

"Whoa, whoa, whoa, hang on," Rett says. "I can explain."

"Fuck you," I spit. I'm so angry, I'm on fire, feeling my cheeks go red with it. "All this time, you made me believe that you were in love with me, but you've got her in your hotel room. I cannot believe you."

"No, you're not listening," he starts.

MacKenzie Taylor comes to the door and I can smell the booze on her from out here. I want to punch both of them right in the mouth, make it so that neither can sing or do whatever they were doing in here alone together.

Instead, I whirl around and start back to the elevators. Gabriela's face is twisted in sympathetic anger.

"No, wait!" Rett calls out. "Nicole."

I flip him off behind me and step into the elevator, still shaking. Gabriela punches at the button for the ground floor.

The doors close as Rett approaches them, still ranting. "Please," he says, but he's cut off as the doors close and we're being trolleyed back to the lobby.

"Well," Gabriela says. "That definitely didn't go the way I thought it would."

I don't respond. Inside, though, I'm screaming.

CHAPTER THIRTY-ONE

Rett

The final three nights of the tour felt like I was just running through the motions, and now that I'm back home, I realize how exhausted I am. Everything went to shit, all at once. Sure, we made a ton of money and we had a ridiculous amount of exposure – hell, at one point, I learned that I was a damn Twitter hashtag, with fan picture accounts and everything – but there's something about the whole experience that feels like we sold our souls to get it.

I haven't heard much from anyone at the label since we got back either. Granted, they're probably trying to put out a dozen fires as it is, with the Van Hope Group under intense media scrutiny. Even if someone from the label had tried to call or email, I've been doing nothing but sleeping and feeling shitty.

I tried to call Nicole when we got back, but it went straight to voicemail. Either her phone is off or she's blocked me. Which sucks. If she doesn't want to hear from me, I can respect that, but I just hate how things went down. It was obvious she came to see me in Baton Rouge for a reason, and when she left without saying anything, without even letting me explain what was going on, I just felt my heart sink. Now there's a permanent hole that exists in my life and I can't do anything to fill it.

The sun is shining through my bedroom windows, making prisms of light that ripple on my sheets. I need coffee.

I get up out of bed, throw on a pair of joggers and a Nashville Sounds t-shirt and go into the open kitchen, where I prepare the coffee maker. After a few minutes, the thing gurgles and spurts and I have a fresh cup in my hands. My bay windows in the living area look down from the loft to the streets below, bustling with Monday morning business. I imagined mornings like this would be spent with Nicole by my side, sipping coffee, and enjoying the start of the day. It feels hauntingly lonely spending them by myself.

My cell phone rings on the kitchen counter, the thing buzzing against the marble surface, and I shuffle over to pick it up. At first, my heart jumps, hoping it's Nicole, knowing I'm home from the tour. Instead, Clay's face is illuminated on the screen, a ridiculous picture I took of him at a New Year's Eve show a couple of years ago.

"What's up?" I say as I put the phone to my ear.

"Good, you're up," he says. "Turn on the TV, right now. Channel 7."

I go over to the couch in the living area and find the television remote, powering on the Samsung mounted on the brick wall.

"What's going on?" I ask.

"You'll see."

"Oh, boy," I sigh.

MacKenzie Taylor's sullen face fills my television screen and I do a double-take. It's not uncommon to see her doing interviews, especially during an album cycle, but her entire countenance, even before I hear her voice, tells me something serious is up.

The ticker at the bottom of the screen reads EXCLU-SIVE: COUNTRY STAR MACKENZIE TAYLOR DETAILS SEXUAL ASSAULT ALLEGATIONS AGAINST MEDIA MOGUL MAX VAN HOPE.

The camera cuts to the interviewer, one of the hosts from the affiliate's morning show. She's an older woman with a refined voice that's like a weighted blanket, soft yet secure. "And what was that like?" she asks. "You find out about all these allegations against Max Van Hope while on tour, knowing that you as well were one of his victims."

"I didn't want to continue the tour, to be honest. It felt like all I was doing at that point was putting money back into the Van Hopes' pocketbooks."

"The pocketbook of the man you allege molested and sexually assaulted you," the interviewer says.

"Yes," MacKenzie nods. Her bottom lip quivers and she looks away for a moment before steeling herself. "I started in this business when I was fifteen years old. I got my first contract with the Van Hope Group two years later. In hindsight, I can see how I was being groomed by Max Van Hope."

"And he was still involved in the operations of the record label, Giant Records, at that time?"

"Oh yes," MacKenzie says. "He was head of A&R."

"And you say that he drugged you with a drink?" the interviewer asks.

"That's right. It was at a record release party, and he gave me a drink. I was still underage at the time, but I wanted to look cool. I took it, and I almost immediately started feeling unwell. Unbalanced. My sight was blurry and even now, the memory is fuzzy. But I woke up the next morning in Max's bed. You can imagine the rest."

"That must have been terrifying."

"It was awful," MacKenzie says. "I went to Laura Van Hope afterward, and confided in her with what had happened. The next day, Max was removed from the label and placed as the head of their family's modeling firm."

"And it was while you were on tour that you saw the news reports about these most recent allegations against him? What made you continue?" the host asks. "What gave you the strength to play through these recent concerts, knowing that there was so much turmoil around the Van Hope family and their brands?"

"Honestly, I was ready to pull the plug, but the frontman for our opening act —"

"Rett Gordon," the interviewer interjects.

"Yeah, Rett," MacKenzie says. "He sat down with me the night that I was ready to call it quits, and he just said that the people we're really doing this for are the fans, the people who pay their hard-earned money to see us in concert. We can't take that joy from them."

I fall onto the couch.

"You still there?" Clay asks.

"Yeah," I say, still holding the phone to my ear. "This seems like it's not going to end well."

"No, it's not. Not for Giant Records and the Van Hope Group, at least," Clay says.

"Yeah, but if they go under, we don't have a contract. No record deal." I feel my stomach drop to my groin and I want to throw up. "Fuck," I say. "What are we going to do?"

"It'll be alright. We have enough money from this tour," he says. "We've got some time to figure it out."

The interviewer leans into MacKenzie and takes her hand. "Thank you for being so brave and for telling your story. There are so many more like you out there, countless others, and I hope they see your strength here."

"Thank you," MacKenzie says.

The interviewer turns to the camera. "When we come back, we've got more on the allegations against Max Van Hope. We'll also hear from one of the models who works for the Van Hope Group who has her own story. Stay tuned."

"Shit," I say as the television cuts to commercials.

"Yeah," Clay says. He breathes heavily into the phone. "This ain't good, brother."

"You're right, it's not." I think about Nicole and Mac-Kenzie and Gabriela, all these women affected by the men around them, these women who now have life-altering scars on their psyche and their hearts. "We need a plan."

"I'll call Chris and Dave. Let's all meet up at the rehearsal space this afternoon. I've got an idea."

"Oh yeah?" I ask.

"Yeah," he says. "It's about twenty percent of an idea, but we can discuss this afternoon what we're going to do next."

"Whatever you say. You're the boss."

He hangs up, the phone going silent. I toss the thing on the kitchen counter and lean against the stained concrete surface, taking a long sip from my coffee.

This is not what I thought we'd be coming back home to, with our entire way of life and our career threatened by one man's choices. My mind immediately goes to hiring an attorney if something drastic happens. We'll need it if we lose our contract or our next tour because of the Van Hope Group.

My head starts pounding from all this nervousness and I grab my phone from the counter. I swipe through to Nicole's number and try to call her again.

It goes straight to voicemail.

CHAPTER THIRTY-TWO

Nico

The front door opens and Gabriela comes in, an air of victory around her like an aura.

"You did so good," I say, getting up from the couch and setting my laptop on the coffee table.

I walk across the living room to her, and I can see through her glow that she's holding something in.

"What is it?" I ask.

"God, it's like you can read me without me even saying anything."

"Well, I've known you since we were kids," I shrug.

"Listen, someone wants to talk with you," she starts.

My brain immediately goes into panic mode. I don't want to talk to him. I learned everything I needed to know about Rett Gordon when I found him with Mac-Kenzie Taylor in his hotel, well after midnight. He's just like every other guy I've ever met. Ready to move on to the next woman who will shower him with attention. I don't want any part of him or what he wants to talk to me about.

"I don't want to talk to Rett," I say haughtily.

"Well, it's not Rett. Just be cool and listen to what she has to say."

Before I can respond, Gabriela opens the front door again, and MacKenzie Taylor is standing on our front step. I've only seen her in person two other times – one of those times was very briefly in Rett's hotel – but she looks older than she has before. Whatever youthful exuberance she portrays on stage, she must have left in the dressing room. There's a heaviness in her eyes that makes me empathize with her. Whether I like her or not, whatever my feelings are, I know that the three of us together right here in this entryway all know the same pain.

"Hi," she says.

"Hi," I respond.

Gabriela between us begins to mediate. "When we were at the news studio, we got to talking, and there's something you need to hear, Nicole."

"Okay."

"Why don't we go sit down?" Gabriela says, motioning to the couch in the living room.

"I feel like I've done a lot of that lately," MacKenzie says. "I don't want to take too much of your time. I just want you to know that whatever you think of Rett, whatever you think you saw when you came to the hotel, it's not what it is. If anything, Rett saved my life that night."

I purse my lips. I am ready to put Rett Gordon, and Nashville altogether, in my rearview. I finally got word that I've been accepted to the position in Missoula. I'm packing up my things and going back home.

Gabriela motions once again to the living room, and I capitulate. "Alright," I say. "Let's talk."

We go to the living room and take a seat on the couch. I sit in the brown leather chair that's positioned perpendicular to the couch, with my feet pulled up underneath me.

"I'm sure you saw the news this morning," MacKenzie says. "Being able to tell my truth to the world has been so liberating, but I see how my behavior has affected the people around me. I had – and have – this ridiculous need to please the people around me, and to hoard their attention. I recognize it for what it is – a coping mechanism. Coping with what happened to me."

I nod. "I know what you mean. It's easy to fall into that."

"I'll admit, my behavior toward Rett was part of that," she continues. "I had this weird fixation on being seen with him, being seen together, to make the paparazzi and the blogs talk, because I knew it would draw interest in my brand. Even if I didn't actually want to date him, I knew that just the speculation would cause a media frenzy. I've been told for years that's all that matters – that the media make or break a career, and you do whatever you can to stay in their camera lens."

"He's a good guy," I say. "You'd be lucky to be with him."

"No," she says. "Well, yes. He's a good guy. He's a great guy. I was vulnerable, feeling down, and terrible. Any other guy would've found me in that state and taken the opportunity to sleep with me. And you know what? I would have let them. Anything to bury that pain. But not Rett. He never tried to make a move, he never tried to take advantage of me. He sat and listened to me. And he told me how much he misses you. He is so in love with you, Nico. And I'm sorry that I messed that up for you in any way."

A lump catches in my throat. I don't know what to say. I wanted to completely let go of Rett, and forget about Nashville. I know all I was doing was running from the most hurt and shame I've ever felt. And now, here in front of me, are two women who faced their hurt head-on. As proud of them as I am, I am ashamed of myself.

"Nicole," Gabriela speaks up. "Don't run away from this. It's okay."

She's always been able to read my mind, like she's got some kind of sixth sense.

"I'm not," I say. "I'm tired of running."

"Good," she says.

"For what it's worth," MacKenzie says, "and I'm sorry that it's so late coming out, but I'm sorry for how I behaved toward Rett in front of you."

I purse my lips as I recall the images of her practically hanging off of him at the Nashville Sounds baseball game a few months ago.

She continues, "I was just so obsessed with staying in the spotlight, making sure I gave plenty for the gossip blogs to talk about. Isn't that so disgusting?" She looks off for a moment, and I can see tears forming in the corners of her eyes. "I was just feeding that beast without realizing that I was giving up myself."

"I'm sure it's an easy cycle to get caught up in," I say.

"It is. And then I had the Van Hopes constantly telling me about how I needed more and more media exposure, that I needed to stay relevant. Ha!" She laughs heavily now, one step ahead of her tears.

"You're incredibly brave," I say. "Both of you."

Gabriela takes my hand and gives it a loving squeeze.

"Thank you," I say. "To both of you. And I'm sorry for despising you, MacKenzie. I know you didn't deserve that. When I found out Rett was going on tour with you, I hated you so much."

"I understand," she says.

"I'm glad he was there to take care of you when you needed someone. Maybe that's the universe's way of providing you with someone strong enough to take on your burdens when you can't, you know?"

"Yeah," she says. "I like that."

It was that kind of caring and loving Rett has always shown, ever since I met him. From getting me to the hospital when Gabriela had her emergency surgery, to taking care of his dad's blown-down fence, to making sure Mac-

Kenzie was alright during her breakdown, he has constantly been a provider. I can't let that go.

I am in love with him.

Allowing myself to finally feel that love puts a warmth in my chest that grows until my whole body is radiating from it. I smile and then laugh. Both Gabriela and MacKenzie look at me, concerned.

"I'm okay," I say, giggling still. "It's just…I'm in love with a country music star."

* * *

After MacKenzie leaves and I make sure Gabriela isn't snooping, I pull out my cell phone and find the contact I'm looking for. He answers within a couple of rings.

"Hey," he says. "Long time no see. Or talk. Or whatever."

"Yeah," I say, almost guiltily. "Rett's not with you is he?"

"No, but he's supposed to be here any minute."

"Well, listen. I need your help with something."

"Talk to me."

I tell him my plan.

"It's perfect," he says. "I'm in. I'll get everything together on my end."

We hang up and I smile, excited for what's to come.

CHAPTER THIRTY-THREE

Rett

We're in our rehearsal space, the only place that feels like home right now. As our entire world and support system falls apart around us, the guys decided that our meeting should be held here instead of in some conference room somewhere.

I look around the place, all the dreams we've had of recording our new album here. Bringing in a producer and doing it all in this space, was a dream nearly realized. Now? Who knows what happens next. The entire Van Hope Group is under scrutiny, with not only the allegations of Max's sexual misconduct, but with it coming to light that Laura helped cover it up.

I wish, at this moment, that we'd never signed with them. It was such a lucrative deal but now I wish we'd stayed independent. At least then our fate would have been in our own hands.

The four of us are sitting in a circle amongst the instruments. Chris is leaning back in his chair, trying to balance it on two legs. Clay is texting with someone and Dave returns to his chair with a freshly-made green smoothie in one hand and a pile of almonds in the other.

We're waiting for David, our A&R rep at Giant Records. After our emergency meeting yesterday, we decided that before we could do anything else, we needed to get with him to find out what our options are. He responded to my email immediately, saying he wanted to have an urgent, confidential meeting with us. All of us know what that means, though.

Get ready to get dropped by the label.

I am sweating, and I can feel the back of my linen button-up sticking to my body as it's sandwiched between my skin and the leather seat. It feels like we're all sitting ducks waiting around for an execution.

Every single possible scenario runs through my head. If Giant drops us, we still have the material for an album and the space to record. Thanks to the tour, we have the money to self-produce, but that's essentially a death sentence. Sure, we'll continue playing the Nashville circuit, and perhaps college campuses, but we won't have the large audiences like we had over this last tour. We'll be relegated to the list of flame-outs, the could-have-beens.

As all of these things bombard my thoughts, all I want is Nicole. I want to wrap my arms around her and feel her tight against me, her comfort and warmth melting away all this nervousness and anxiety.

"You alright over there?" Clay asks, waving his hand in my face.

I'm in a daze. Blinking myself back to the present moment, I reply, "Yeah. Just ready to get this over with so we know where to go next."

"I feel ya." He tosses me a silver bullet, and I crack it open. If there's ever been a time for beer, it's now.

As we discuss the problems with the Van Hope Group, there's a knock at the door.

Clay gets up to answer it, and David and another guy walk in. Every time I've ever seen David during business hours, he's in a suit and tie. Today, he's wearing a vest with no jacket and a pair of jeans. His counterpart, who I've never met before, is similarly dressed. It's professional without being too formal, and it works. For some reason, my anxieties ease. Maybe because they're not dressed as pallbearers.

"Hey, guys," David says, stepping into the rehearsal loft. He takes a moment to observe the place. "Wow. This is quite the recording studio."

I stand from my chair to go to shake his hand. "We wanted something that didn't feel sterile, a space that would help nurture creativity. Plus, we can save money using our own place instead of renting out a recording studio."

"That's really smart. That's what I've always liked about you guys," he says. Turning to his counterpart, he introduces the man, who's got short-cropped hair and about a week's worth of stubble on his chiseled jaw. He looks like he could be a model, and he's seemingly not much older than the rest of us – a few years out of college at most. "Guys, I want you to meet a friend of mine. This is Aaron Shipley. We were frat brothers and he's now a contract attorney here in town."

Oh boy, I think. He brought a contract attorney to go over the dissolution of our contract with Giant. We're essentially unemployed. My stomach bottoms out and the Coors Light that I drank before feels like it's going to come up my esophagus. How everything went from perfect to a train wreck so quickly has given me emotional whiplash. More than that, it's the fact that we had nothing to do with it – that our destiny as a band is completely under the thumb of a corporation who is having to put out self-lit fires left and right.

"What do you say we all take a seat and go over some things?" David says.

Clay, ever the consummate host, leads David and Aaron to our poker table, where we usually sit to shoot the shit. We all take a seat around the table. Aaron has brought a briefcase that he's had tucked under his arm. He flips it open and pulls out a stack of papers.

This is it.

"Okay," David starts. "First and foremost, let's get this out of the way. Giant is in trouble. Big trouble. But also, you are under contract, and to void the contract, they'd either have to pay you severance or you'd have to buy your way out. So, your position within Giant's repertoire is not under threat here, as long as you're okay with knowing you're on the Titanic, and the iceberg has just fucked everything up."

This gets a nervous laugh from the four of us. But, one of the things I've always appreciated about David, even when he was courting us to sign with Giant three years ago, was his cut-through-the-bullshit style of negotiation. It reminds me a lot of my dad.

He continues, "But let's say you want the contract voided. Who knows how long it will take for them to pay you. If they file bankruptcy, you could be waiting for years in limbo. Unable to sign with anyone else, unable to release music. That said, I think you have a rare and incredible opportunity in front of you, which is why I brought Aaron."

David gestures to Aaron, who clears his throat. "There's no way around it, the entire Van Hope Group is going under. There's no way they can pay all this litigation or settlements without filing for bankruptcy. I wish people had listened to us before, but we've seen this coming for a long time."

My eyebrows perk up and I turn to David. "You've known about this?"

"Of course, man, who hasn't? Max Van Hope is the biggest philanderer this town has ever seen. There were rumors about him and MacKenzie nearly five years ago. When I voiced my concerns after Max was shifted to the promotional and advertising company, I was handed an

NDA. That's when I started planning my exit, and I hooked up with Aaron here to get things rolling."

"So you're leaving Giant?"

"Absolutely. As should you guys." David meets my stare with seriousness. "Right now, Rett Gordon is the name of a hero. The way MacKenzie gushed about you all over television, I'm surprised you can even get out of your apartment without a swarm of news people wanting an interview."

"Well, I've pretty much been holed up here," I mumble.

"What I'm saying is, we have an opportunity to do something big," David says.

"In short," Aaron speaks up, "we're forming our own label." He hands us all a packet of papers stapled together. At the top, the front page is labeled Broadway Records Business Plan.

"We want you," David says. "We want Rett Gordon and The Last Train Home on our roster."

"No offense, David, you know I like you," I say. "But why would we sign with an upstart indie label? We might as well self-produce at this point."

"And you're welcome to do that," David says. "But I've got over a decade in this industry, and all the contacts within it. Which means even though we're an indie label, we've already got distribution and promotional deals in place. I'm talking, Universal, Sony, even overseas stuff. We just need the talent."

"What about MacKenzie? Are you taking her too? Are

we just going to be Giant with a new paint job?" I ask.

"MacKenzie's too big for us already. She's getting offers from Sony and Warner as it is. But, no, we're completely different from Giant, specifically in the structure of the company."

"On that note," Aaron chimes in again, "if you flip to page B-17 in your packets, you'll see our proposed financial structure."

The four of us ruffle through the pages. Though a lot of it is Greek to me, I know Chris understands what he's reading.

Chris looks up from the paper and I can see almost literal dollar signs in his eyes. "You're 100% artist-owned?"

"That's right," David says with a smile.

"So how will you make money?" I ask.

"The profit structure is on the next page, but essentially, we'll take a cut from tickets, merch, and music downloads. A small cut, but enough to pay salaries and marketing."

I turn the page and nearly fall out of my chair. "You want to give us 60% take on tours?"

"Not give you. You make the money. We just ask for 40% in return."

"This is too good to be true," I say.

"Well, there is one catch," David says, pursing his lips. "You're still under contract with Giant."

"But," Aaron says, "David gave me a copy of the contract you guys signed. You have one record left on the deal, though there's a buyout clause at that point. It's fifty grand."

David smiles. "Didn't you guys just take Daniel Valencia for eight percent on this last tour? Surely you can afford your freedom." He nods to the silver bullet in front of me. "As long as you haven't spent it all on cheap beer already."

I look to Clay and to Dave – who's still nose-deep in the financials of the business plan – and to Chris. There's the unspoken understanding about what to do next.

"You can stay on the sinking ship, or you can buy a fifty-thousand-dollar lifeboat," David says. "It's your choice, but the longer you are associated with the Van Hopes, the more your emotional capital with the public goes away, whether it's fair or not."

I know he's right, which sucks. However, we've got an open window here.

"I've got some requests before I even begin to think about saying yes," I say.

"Let's hear them," David says.

"First, I want a portion of our proceeds to go to victims of sexual assault. Women's groups, stuff like that."

"Done."

"Second, I want you to offer Nico St. John a job as a songwriting consultant. Someone who can help the artists on the roster with their music. She was irreplaceable with our new album."

"Already done."

"Really?" I ask.

"She's our next meeting actually."

"Good."

"I have a request," Chris pops up.

"Give it to me," David says.

"Whatever bus company you use for tours, we want better beds," Chris says.

We all laugh.

"Well, we won't be using the Van Hopes' people," David says. "Anything else?"

The guys and I turn to each other, doing that unspoken grunt-and-shrug thing.

"Nope, that's it," I say.

"Well, first thing's first, Aaron is going to help you with buying out your contract from Giant. We'll prepare everything for pushing out the new album, and we'll get a press release together."

"I have another idea," Clay says.

"Shoot," David nods.

"Instead of a press release or a press conference, let's do a concert. We'll make it our announcement and we'll donate the door to the Downtown Women's Center," Clay says.

"I love that idea," David says. "Rett?"

I nod. "Yeah, I love it," I say. "It's a fantastic idea."

"Alright." David stands and raps his knuckles on the felt surface of the poker table. "We've got a lot of work to do. Let's roll."

CHAPTER THIRTY-FOUR

Rett

Chris hits the bass drum and it rattles my chest. I never get tired of that feeling. Even with the in-ear monitors helping keep the mix down and protecting my hearing, I love feeling that bass drum as it thumps. It makes me feel the music, more than just hear it.

The lights come up on stage and, after a four count, the entire band rips into one of the songs from our last album. The crowd roars in response. Lasers and fog machines are going full blast.

The house is packed. Absolutely packed. Thanks to some good press and our new marketing team at Broadway Records, everything has been going incredibly smooth. Giant let us out of our contract – with the fifty-thousand-dollar payment, of course – and we were brought on board with David and Aaron.

I've always known that David was meant for big things, and I can see him out in the crowd enjoying himself. He was the very first person to take a shot on us, and now we've done the same with his new label. Despite the whirlwind and the aftermath of the Van Hope Group situation, he's been able to keep things going steady with the new place.

Though I was hesitant and scared at first, if the ticket sales for this one-off concert are any indication of what the future is going to be like with the entire team at Broadway, we've got nothing to worry about.

We finish the opening song of the set to a raucous applause.

"How's it going Nashville?" I call out into the microphone.

Again, a wave of cheers and high-pitched screams meet the stage, nearly flooring me.

"Thank you all for coming out tonight. This is a special night for us, and we can't do it without any of you. But more importantly, we're here tonight to show support for the women in our lives who have been affected by sexual assault. If you're anything like me, you know someone who's had her life upturned. Thankfully there are resources and help out there, which is why we're donating the entire door to the Downtown Women's Center."

Again, a huge applause fills the air.

"Spending the last six months writing and recording our new album – which is due out in two months from

Broadway Records, by the way – I got to spend a lot of time with an incredibly special woman. This record wouldn't be what it is without her influence. This next song goes out to Nico St. John, wherever she may be."

I start strumming the chords to the song, with the band coming in behind me after eight measures. It's a slow ballad, and Dave is playing with a glass slide. As I come back up to the microphone, the stage spotlight moves out to the crowd. I watch as it scans and it lands on a man standing in the middle of the audience. I see his face, his smile, and my voice catches in my throat.

There he is, a few rows back, beaming up at me.

"Dad?" I say into the microphone.

I turn to Clay, who's just looking at me with a wide grin across his lips. He nods and gives me a little wink.

My mind is completely empty. My dad standing in the middle of a concert audience is something I've never seen before. As I turn back to him, he smiles, and lifts his hands above his head. He unrolls a cardboard sign.

She loves you, it reads in thick Sharpie.

My eyebrows furrow. The band continues to play, but I'm dumbstruck. The sound completely silenced in my head, and all I can hear is the pounding of my heart in my chest.

Then, I see her. Nicole. Standing right next to my dad. She holds up a sign of her own.

I love you.

I drop my guitar, and a tech grabs it before the head-stock hits the ground. I don't care though; I jump off the stage. As I do, the crowd erupts in cheers and the security guards at the front of the barrier between them and the stage have to press the people back. I make my way into the audience and swim through them.

As the people in the crowd around me realize what is going on, they all clear a path to my dad and Nicole, who are standing in the middle of a growing empty circle.

"Hey son," my dad says as I reach them. The crow's feet in the corners of his eyes crease as he smiles. "The band sounds really good. I'm proud of you for what you guys are doing here. Donating all that money."

"Thank you." My chin trembles. "I can't believe you came."

"Well, you can thank this young lady right here. I guess she finally talked me into it."

I turn to Nicole.

There are so many emotions running through my brain.

She's here.

She loves me.

She brought my dad.

All of this happiness and surprise feels like it will burst out of my chest in a ray of light.

"Wow," is all that can come out of my lips.

"Rett, I am so sorry," she says. There are tears in her eyes too. "I was so stupid, and I did what I always do. I tried to run away because I was scared. But you—"

I cup her cheeks in my hands and pull her into me, kissing her with all the love in my soul. Nicole wraps her arms around the back of my neck and kisses me back. The entire concert venue cheers.

I pull away for a moment. "By the way," I say. "I love you too."

Nicole smiles and pulls me in for another kiss.

The crowd goes wild.

EPILOGUE

Nico

I wake up, the sheets wrapped around my otherwise nude body. My clothes are on the floor, but over the last six weeks, I've been smart and made sure to keep some loungewear here at Rett's. It's been a whirlwind of a month, too. The guys have finished the album, and it was released to rave reviews. I haven't even seen Gabriela except in passing. She's been giving talks at the universities and schools in the area about sexual assault survival, and she's booked up through the next three months.

I've also filed my formal complaint with both the university and the department head in Texas, and he's been placed on administrative leave pending the investigation. The work isn't done, but finally, I'm not running away from it.

When David offered me a job with his upstart record

label, I immediately accepted it, and rescinded my application with the University of Montana. Despite the drama around what went down with the Van Hope Group, this has been the most rewarding experience of my career.

Plus, by choosing to stay in Nashville, I get to wake up to Rett Gordon nearly every morning.

I turn over to kiss Rett good morning, but he's already out of bed, the sheets and duvet tucked tightly into his side. Reaching for my phone on the bedside table, I check the time. It's just after 9am. As my senses come to me, I can smell coffee. And bacon.

I find a pair of yoga pants and a t-shirt in the closet and walk from the bedroom into the kitchen, pulling my hair into a ponytail.

"You know, besides the incredible sex, my favorite thing about being with you is the breakfast the next morning," I say.

He's at the stove, his back turned to me. He's got on a white t-shirt that accentuates his muscles and his favorite pair of grey fleece joggers, his usual morning attire.

"Well," he says. He moves to the coffee maker and pours me a mug. "Stick with me and there will be plenty of both."

"Promise?" I wink.

"Oh my god," he laughs. "Did you just try to wink?"

"What?" I say. "I'm trying to be sexy."

"I know." Rett comes around the counter and wraps me in his arms.

"How do you always smell so good?" I ask, my face

pressed to his chest.

"It's an entire adolescence of chopping wood. My skin is infused with cedar."

"Or you just have really good cologne."

"Or that," he says.

He lets me go and returns to the stove, transferring strips of bacon to a paper towel-lined platter.

"Big plans today?" he asks over his shoulder.

"Not really."

"What would you say if we spend the day bringing more of your stuff over here?" he asks. He turns and leans against the counter. "Maybe make it a more permanent thing?"

My eyes dart up. "Are you asking me to move in with you?"

"Yeah. I am," he says. "I mean, you're here most of the week anyway, and…"

I grin and cut him off. "I think that sounds great."

"Okay," he says. He winks at me and I laugh.

"You're never allowed to make fun of me again for winking," I say.

He laughs and turns his attention back to the stove top.

I pull out my phone to tell Gabriela the news and scroll my notifications and news feed. There's one that makes me nearly jump out of my seat.

"Have you looked at your phone this morning?" I ask.

Rett turns, concerned. "What? No. Why? Is everything okay?"

"Oh yes," I say. "But you're going to flip." I walk over to the stove and show him the screen, which is open to the week's Billboard charts.

With Rett Gordon and The Last Train Home's new album, *Love Through the War*, debuting at #1.

He grabs my phone and his eyes go wide.

"Holy shit!" he exclaims. Picking me up, he twirls me around and kisses me, deep and long.

"I'm so proud of you," I say.

"Proud of us," he responds. "Proud of us. This record would have been nothing without you. You are everything to me."

I wrap my legs tighter around his hips, feeling him press against me.

"How do you feel about cold bacon?" he asks, kissing my neck, nuzzling his lips against my skin. It makes my whole body shiver with excitement.

"I love it," I say with a smile as he carries me to our bedroom.

THE END

Clay will return in

You've Got the Music in You

Available February 2022!

ACKNOWLEDGEMENTS

At the beginning of his career, Stephen King's publisher told him that it would be unacceptable to publish more than one book per year, that the reading public would find his brand diluted. Therefore, King convinced the suits at Signet to publish a few of his novels under the pseudonym Richard Bachman.

J.K. Rowling is most known for the *Harry Potter* series, but she also writes detective novels under the pen name Robert Galbraith.

J.D. Robb is actually Norah Roberts.

Why did I choose a *nom de plume* for this book? Well, the answer is complicated.

I love romance. I love the genre and the happy-ever-afters and all the swoon-worthy moments. Even though you know in an HEA novel that the characters will end up together, (otherwise, it wouldn't be a *happy ever after*) it's the journey, the obstacles that they have to overcome, both externally and internally, that make me keep turning the page. After writing a half-dozen novels, mostly thriller/mystery, I wanted to try my pen at romance and

HEA.

I believe we all see the world through our own little key-hole, and that keyhole is shaped by our experiences in life. For me, I've never known political intrigue. I've never been around a lot of guns or violence. I don't know how to fly a helicopter. But my life has been full of drama. Of love and heartbreak. I'm a child of divorce. I've struggled and I've had lucky breaks and I've fallen in love. Despite some of the thrillers and mysteries that I've written, my keyhole is shaped like a romance novel. Those are the experiences that have made me who I am, and make me see the world the way I do.

When I set out to write this story, I knew immediately, before even writing the first chapter, that it would be a project set apart from my standard Andrew J Brandt novels. Frankly, if I released an HEA romance novel under the AJB name, it would probably confuse – and most likely piss off – a large contingent of my reader base who expect page-turning mystery. A pseudonym was paramount.

This is also stylistically different from anything else I've ever done. It's first-person, told from two perspectives and it's present-tense. These are hallmarks of modern romance, and completely different from how I "normally" write. It couldn't be AJB. It had to be something different. It had to be Elliott Andrews.

If you've picked up this book because you like romance, thank you for spending your hard-earned dollars on what is essentially my debut novel. There are a ton of established and talented writers in the romance genre, and there are many who are head-and-shoulders better at it than I am, but thank you.

If you are coming at this as a fan of Andrew J Brandt, thank you as well. I hope you are able to read this with an open mind and understanding that this isn't a thriller or a mystery, but a sweet love story that was a ton of fun to write.

As always, there are a ton of people to thank here. Jennifer, thank you for believing in me and for always being so supportive. You were the very first person to read this story (outside of myself) and knowing that you liked it made me know that it was worth publishing. I love you.

Huge kudos to:

Gabe Morgan
Morgan Duerden
Rachael McClung
Derek Porterfield

Brandon Biggers
Andrew Monroe
Travis Tidmore
Burrowing Owl Books

Charles D'Amico
LaMyiah Harvel
Dallas Bell
Rick Treon
Abby Jimenez
Jen Morris
Kenny Nagunst
Melissa Grace
Sam Finn
The Smoke Easy Guys

Rodrigo Godoy
Raphael McHenry
Jeremiah Cunningham
Jered Lopez
Jim Livingston
Kaleb West
Drew Gibson
Lyssa Kay Adams
Gordon Clark

ABOUT THE AUTHOR

Elliott Andrews is the coffee-addicted, notebook-hoarding, romance-writing pseudonym of award-nominated and #1 bestselling author Andrew J Brandt.

All the Right Notes is his first romance novel.

Find more information online at
www.elliottandrews.com

Made in the USA
Columbia, SC
23 July 2021